The Last Great ADVENTURE of the PB&J SOCIETY

by
JANET SUMNER JOHNSON

Capstone Young Readers
a Capstone Imprint

The Last Great Adventure of the PB&J Society
is published by
Capstone Young Readers
A Capstone Imprint
1710 Roe Crest Drive
North Mankato, MN 56003
www.mycapstone.com

Cataloging-in-Publication Data is available on the
Library of Congress website.

978-1-62370-636-4 (US paper over board)
978-1-4965-2695-3 (US library binding)
978-1-4965-2697-7 (US ebook PDF)

Printed in China.
092015   009215S16

*For my mom, who read my first draft and
had the courage to tell me to keep working.*

For my dad, who taught me to love PB&Js.

*And for Rick, whose encouragement and
support made this all possible.*

I snuck the phone into the hall closet, where Kate's faux fur parka would muffle the sound. I hit speed-dial #7 and let it ring once, then hung up and called again. Our secret code. It rang twice before Jason answered.

"Annie?"

"I've got a body count." I was all business. "Burial required pronto."

"Like, now?"

"Affirmative. See you in five."

"Wait!" Jason coughed. "The parental units admitted an unknown onto the premises. Emergency mission in progress. Need more time. Repeat. Need more time."

"*Jason*, this is important. I'm coming. You have five." I hung up.

Much more possibility of getting caught this way, but Jason was stubborn. If I waited for him to come on his own, it might never happen.

I listened for the telltale sounds of danger — like Kate, bane-of-my-existence slash big-sister-from-Hades, coming home from school — then slipped out of the closet and replaced the phone. I slunk to my room and extracted the pre-packed bag from under my bed.

I hated to break cover, but if I didn't check in, I'd be grounded. Still, my timing couldn't be better. Mom was like a zombie on bills day. I poked my head into her room.

"I'm going to Jason's."

She didn't even turn around. "Have fun. Dinner's at six."

Avoiding the creaky spots, I raced downstairs. I reached for the doorknob, only to be whacked as the door flew open.

"Watch it, squirt!" Kate glared as though *I* had hit *her*.

I rubbed my soon-to-be-bruised arm and tried to scoot past. Being on a mission, I even bit back my reply. I needed out before Kate compromised my position.

Kate's mouth twisted into a grin.

Too late.

"Where are you going, anyway? To your *boyfriend's*?"

I clutched my bag tight and stood as tall as I could. "He's *not* my boyfriend!"

Kate laughed as she pushed past. "Right."

I stomped outside, cringing as the door banged shut. So much for my cover.

Stupid sister.

But I forced myself to unclench my fists. I wasn't in the clear yet and needed to be alert. Enemy spies could be anywhere.

Bag over my shoulder, I slowed to a casual stroll and whistled as I scanned the area. Across the cul-de-sac, Mrs. Schuster — a.k.a. Mrs. Meany — pulled weeds from her perfect flower garden. The old woman eyed me, and I looked away.

Next door, Billy pedaled on his trike while his mom watched from the garage. A picture of innocence. But was it? I kept up my guard.

For a lesser spy, the pressure might have been too much, but Jason and I had been working on our technique for three years now. Ever since he got that spy kit for his seventh birthday.

I knew what to do. Breathing in the warm September air, I hitched up my pack, then whistled all casual-like until I rounded the corner house. When the coast was clear, I sprinted the rest of the way to Jason's.

As always, Mr. Parker's beat-up truck sat in the driveway. Lumber jutted from the back as though Jason's dad was headed to his next framing job, like it had for a while now. A shiny off-white Lexus was parked at the curb.

That must belong to the intruder.

I rang the doorbell and put on my best especially-for-adults smile. Turkeys squawked in Jason's backyard, and I jumped. I hated those things!

Mr. Parker started raising turkeys a few years ago as a hobby. I think Jason's mom had been on some organic kick back then. But so many people had begged to buy one of his "organic" turkeys for the holidays, he'd gone all serious about it. I really wish he would have consulted me first.

In the last few weeks he'd sold off more than half, though not enough for my tastes.

Still, I managed to be polite when Mrs. Parker answered the door.

"Hello, Annie dear. Let me go get Jason." She frowned a little, brushed back a strand of her curly dark hair, and glided toward Jason's room.

Mrs. Parker looked and dressed more like a model than a mom. Today's outfit was my favorite — sleek black slacks and a sparkly sweater that swooped at the neck. The ruby choker she usually wore with it was gone, as were the clangy bracelets, but she still looked beautiful. I tried to imagine myself in such an outfit, but . . . it just wouldn't be the same with my frizzy hair and freckles.

From the doorway, I saw Mr. Parker and a skinny, blond-bobbed woman at the table in the kitchen. A Tootsie Pop with a wig. They both stared at some papers.

When Mrs. Parker scooted Jason around the corner, Jason tapped his wrist as if he had a watch. He wanted more time. I shrugged and he slipped away to stand by his dad, using one of our practiced evasive tactics.

"So what *is* all this, Dad? It all looks really important."

"Can't you see we're busy?" Mr. Parker barked, then waved him away. "Now go play and let us finish."

I nearly tumbled down the steps. Jason's dad was usually pretty cool. He was the one playing catch with us in the yard — the turkey-free *front* yard — while my dad worked late.

"I don't . . ." Jason tried to stall again, but his mom hustled him to the door.

"You two go have fun." Mrs. Parker spoke a little too brightly. "Be back in time for dinner."

Jason kicked the porch rail before clomping down the steps. "I was this close to completing the mission." He indicated a PB&J-sized gap between his thumb and pointer finger.

I shrugged again. "She's probably nobody important. Parents invite strange people over all the time."

"I don't know. Things have been . . . *weird* lately, and I bet she's involved."

I was about to ask what he meant, but something glinted in the Pierces' window across the street. "Oh no! Lila. Hurry before she sees us!" I picked up the pace but Jason didn't follow.

"We could throw her off our track by cutting through my backyard." He moved toward the gate.

My stomach dropped and my palms went clammy. The gobbling got louder. He couldn't be serious. Then I saw the wicked grin on his face.

"Jason Parker! That is not funny. Those . . . *things* back there are dangerous." I stomped in the other direction.

Jason ran to catch up. "All right, all right. I'm sorry. But Lila's not that bad, you know."

I shook my head. "Are you kidding? Need I remind you what happened last time I agreed to hang out with her?" I grabbed a fistful of my still-uneven hair as evidence of her horridness. "And anyway, we're going to the *cemetery*. Remember?"

Jason cracked a smile. "I still can't believe you *let* her touch your hair with scissors. I mean, you could have said no."

I scowled at him. He knew the story — he should be more sympathetic. She'd wiled me into her lair with the latest video games, then enticed me with a signed poster of my favorite soccer player — I'm still mad my mom didn't let me keep it. Anyway, he would have done it too if it had been him. "Let's just hurry."

We sprinted to the garden at the side of my house and slipped into our secluded patch between the corn and the cherry tree.

Every spring, with the forced labor of Kate, Matt, and I, my mom planted a giant of a garden — the biggest in the neighborhood. It spread from the house all the way to the ditch and had a little of everything. But the best part was the five full rows of corn next to the big fat cherry tree. They made the perfect hiding spot in summer and fall, which Jason and I turned into an unmarked cemetery.

This side of my house had no windows, so no one could spy on us from above. And not wanting to hurt the roots, my mom never planted anything too close to the tree. The graves wouldn't be disturbed.

I dropped to my knees, bag in front, and lifted out the dead peanut butter and jelly sandwich. Though two of the edges looked like normal bread crust, the center was smushed flat. Purple jelly spots seeped through the now-gray bread. It definitely qualified according to the rules.

"The two-liter of soda fell on it," I explained, handing it over.

Since we started the cemetery four years ago — after a tragic incident involving a fanny pack, an orange, rock jumping, and several falls — we had scrupulously followed the SPB&J (Smushed Peanut Butter and Jelly) Burial Rules. And Rule #1 was clear: Thou shalt bury all smushed peanut butter and jelly sandwiches, which are unfit to eat, in the secret cemetery.

"How old is it?" Jason asked.

"Just a day. I saved it from the trash when my mom wasn't looking."

Jason wrinkled his nose, eyeing the sandwich. "Aren't we getting too old for this?"

"Too old for what?" I demanded. "Fun?"

I couldn't believe those words had come out of his mouth. He sounded like my mom. Or worse, Kate. Why should we have to be all serious, just because we were ten?

Jason shrugged. "It's just a question."

I huffed. Sat up straight. "I hereby call this meeting of the PB&J Society to order. Let the ceremony begin."

No way Jason wouldn't do his part.

We locked into a staring contest. I didn't breathe until he pulled the sandwich from the baggie and performed the inspection. He turned it frontward and backward and then rotated it to check the sides.

"I hereby pronounce this sandwich mold-free and worthy of burial."

Thanks to a peanut butter and jelly sandwich Jason found squished at the back of his school desk last year, we'd added Rule #6: Thou shalt not bury any sandwich with any non–peanut butter and jelly growths in the cemetery.

Some things were just too gross.

With my mom's gardening spade, I dug a sandwich-sized hole, then winked at Jason. Rule #2: Thou shalt not speak during the ceremony, except the official sermon.

Jason held up the sandwich, then squinched up his face and looked away before I could do my part.

"Time-out," I said. Rule #5: If an emergency shall arise, thou shalt call a time-out to allow speaking. "Don't be such a drama king. I haven't missed in *ages*."

Jason shook his head. "You missed *last* time it was your turn. *And* the time before that."

"And like I said, that was ages ago. Time-in."

Jason raised his eyebrows but held still. I formed a wad of saliva in my mouth and then spit on the sandwich with everything I could muster. I totally didn't miss. Rule #3: Thou shalt spit on the sandwich to give it a taste of what it would have experienced if tragedy hadn't struck.

I laid it in the hole. Then, with hands on our stomachs, we began the special sermon.

"Our dearly beloveds, we are gathered here today to say goodbye to our sandwich." Jason had heard this first part at his grandpa's funeral and insisted it was the only way to begin. I liked how important it sounded.

"We are saddened by the loss of our favorite food and think on happier times before it was smushed and became gross. We are grateful for the many times it saved us from the evils of broccoli casserole and bid it farewell on its new journey to feed the worms. May it rest in peace."

After Jason covered the sandwich with dirt and pounded the mound smooth, we began the official mourning song: "Mary Had a Little Lamb." Rule #4: Thou shalt sing the mourning song after the sandwich is buried.

When we were five and had first planned the burial ceremony, Jason had wanted "Peter, Peter, Pumpkin Eater." He'd just learned to play it on the piano. Being the persuasive person I am, I convinced him "Mary" was much more fitting since Mary and her lamb stick together in the song, just like peanut butter and jelly.

We both wanted to change it but couldn't agree. Jason refused to sing "Wind Beneath My Wings" (perfect, no?), and I refused to sing anything by some band called the Beatles, classic or not. Seriously, why would you name your group after a bug?

To finish up, we put a hand over our heart for a final moment of silence.

When the time was up, I stood, but Jason didn't move. He stared at a stalk of corn as though in a trance.

I nudged him. "Jason?"

He looked up. "Maybe I should go home."

"But we still have an hour. And tomorrow we've got soccer, and Thursday is piano lessons."

Jason's chipmunk cheeks turned pink. "Sorry. It's just my parents have been arguing a lot about money lately. Seriously, sometimes they're so loud I don't even need the Spy Bud Two Thousand."

The Spy Bud system was a baby monitor hidden in our parents' rooms. Totally useful for finding out the stuff parents want to keep secret. I sat back down. "Wow."

"Yeah. A couple weeks ago Dad yelled something about the bank foreclosing on us. I Googled it, Annie. Not good. It means the bank will take our house away."

I could only stare. This was stuff you heard on the news or in social studies. Not from your best friend.

"So what if the two are connected? What if the lady's from the bank or something? What if it means we're going to have to move?"

I opened my mouth but nothing came out (which *never* happens). He and I had been best friends since birth (well, at least his birth — those two hours in the hospital nursery before Jason arrived were the loneliest two hours of my life). He couldn't move.

"Anyway, I'm going home." Jason got up and pushed past a cornstalk.

"Wait!" I finally found my voice. "I'm going with you. Maybe she's just an insurance salesman or something."

"Maybe." But I could tell Jason didn't believe it.

We went in silence. The distance between our houses had never been longer. And it felt like I carried an elephant on my back every step of the way. Two minutes ago, my world had been perfect . . . well, almost perfect, minus an iPhone . . . now I wondered how I'd live until tomorrow.

When we reached the corner, the wigged Tootsie Pop was in Jason's front yard. She pounded a sign into the grass.

The elephant crashed on top of me, smushing me like a two-liter on a peanut butter and jelly sandwich. I couldn't breathe. Even from a distance, the words on the sign were clear: For Sale.

2

I plopped next to Jason on the cafeteria bench and unpacked my lunch. I lined everything up: two cookies, string cheese, a bag of chips, an apple, and of course, one PB&J sandwich. Okay, technically there was a bag of baby carrots, too, but I don't really count those.

The noise from the table across the aisle (Miss Guppy's class) was on the rise, and none of our class had arrived from the cafeteria line yet. We were alone. Despite what Lila may say, bringing lunch had its perks. I leaned over.

"What'd you find out?"

Jason tapped his plastic fork on the Tupperware container in front of him. He frowned until his forehead could double for a freshly plowed garden. "She wasn't from the bank. Just a real estate agent."

I grinned and slugged him in the arm. "So that's good, right?" A For Sale sign in his yard was bad news any way you looked at it. But if *I* didn't look at the bright side, Jason sure wouldn't. And there's nothing worse than a grumpy best friend.

Jason slumped in his seat. "We're moving to California to live with my aunt and uncle as soon as it sells. I guess they have some big house or something."

I bit my cheek. "So what's our plan? I could . . ."

"One of your plans won't fix *this*, Annie." Jason popped open his lunch and a foul odor assaulted us. Like shin guards at the end of soccer season.

"Whoa." Talk about a conversation stopper. I would have slapped Jason out of his stinker of an attitude in no time flat, but I couldn't think past a stench like that.

I pinched my nose. "What *is* that?"

Jason stabbed a purple bit with his fork then let it drop back down. "Vegetable something. Name a gross vegetable, and it's probably in there." He slunk even farther in his seat.

I recognized the broccoli and lima beans, and the tomato and carrot slices were pretty obvious. It was the streaks of purple and the slimy green and yellow blobs that were a mystery. "I didn't think *anything* could be worse than broccoli casserole. What else you got?" I motioned at the paper sack.

Jason smashed the bag flat. "Nothing. My mom's on some health kick." He poked a carrot slice and stared at it. Squinching his eyes shut, he took a deep breath. His fingers tensed around the fork.

He was actually going to eat it!

It was halfway in his mouth.

"Don't do it!" I said.

Jason jerked the fork away and the carrot flew to the table, sticking in place like a suction cup.

We stared at it, relieved.

"Here." I ripped my sandwich in half (diagonally, according to Society rules) and held it out. "As your friend, I can't let you eat that."

"You sure?" He sat up straighter.

"Duh."

Jason smiled. "Thanks!" He held out his hand for the PB&J shake, but I shook my head. Not in public!

I divvied up the other stuff. "Maybe I should ask my mom to send an extra tomorrow. Just in case."

"Would you?" Jason's grin widened. "*That's* a plan I can get behind."

I frowned. "Just remember, you owe me."

"Awww . . . you guys are so cute." Lila popped onto the seat across from me, nearly bouncing right back out with perkiness. Her blond ringlets hung in two perfect ponytails. She reminded me of one of those miniature poodles that couldn't stop yapping.

Ugh. It's not like she didn't have friends. Why did she always come to torment us?

"Annie, your hair is totally growing in. I almost can't tell anymore."

I forced myself not to touch it. The haircut incident was just one reason of many I did not like this girl.

"So is it official yet? Are you two going together?"

"What does that even mean?" I snapped.

"You know — boyfriend, girlfriend. You spend all your time together anyway, so you might as well announce it so we can all . . ."

"He's *not* my boyfriend." I got enough of that from Kate. Last thing I needed was for Lila to start some vicious rumor.

Jason scootched to the far edge of his seat. His face was bright red.

"Oh." Lila tilted her head and squinted at us. Finally she opened her milk with a little shrug. "Still. You two *are* cute together."

Jessica and Jenny sat down on either side of Lila. The twins wore matching purple sweat suits with their names bedazzled down the sleeve. Double ugh.

Jason and I shared a look. We needed to finish and finish fast. We concentrated on stuffing our faces while Lila talked. And *man* could she talk.

"So did you see my earrings?" Lila turned her head to show off a diamond stud. Jess and Jen oohed. "They're real, of course. I asked for a new iPhone because who knew you're not supposed to take them in the shower? I mean, they cost enough, you'd think they'd be waterproof. But anyway, Daddy said there's a new version coming out soon, so he didn't want . . ."

Did Lila even hear herself? Seriously, how could the other girls listen to this without gagging? Yet Jess and Jen sat there nodding like bobble heads as though she spoke gospel or something.

An image of that For Sale sign floated through my mind, and I choked on my cookie. If Jason moved, this was what I'd be stuck with.

I nudged Jason, ready to bolt out to recess, when Lila changed the subject.

"Oh, Jason. When we were standing in line, I noticed your jeans are fraying in the seat. I wanted to tell you because I know *I* would want someone to tell me so I could get to the mall pronto . . . unless . . ." Her eyes widened and she covered her mouth. "I forgot. Your dad doesn't have a job. You probably can't afford a new pair. You live so close, I just think you're normal like us." She turned to Jess. "That's why I am so totally going to college some day. And my future husband has to, too, because I refuse to be poor."

Jason's cheeks flamed. He gripped his half-eaten PB&J so hard that I was afraid we'd have to bury the rest. I couldn't let them treat a member of the Society like that.

I was about to tow Jason away when I caught sight of his uneaten lunch.

Lightbulb moment. It was all too perfect. Lila would never see it coming. She was too busy blabbering on about her future career as an interior designer.

Jason grabbed my arm like he could read my mind. After all these years, he probably could. "Annie, forget it."

I shook him off, snatched the container of Vegetable Yuck, but before I could launch it, Jason knocked it from my hand.

It splattered all over us. Everyone jumped back from the table as though it might contaminate them. I couldn't really blame them. With all the different colored chunks, it totally looked like puke.

Jason was on his feet, his arms hanging like a scarecrow's. I wanted to die. I tried to wipe it off, but it clung to me like snot.

It didn't take long for the laughter to start — a whole cafeteria of kids pointing and laughing. Except Lila. She stuffed a wad of napkins at me and acted all nice.

"I'll go get more." And she turned tail.

The phony. I bet she was off to tell on me.

Our teacher's high heels clicked across the cafeteria. "What happened here?"

Jason uttered some apology about his clumsiness, which Mrs. Starry totally bought. We wiped off as much of the goo as we could, then followed her to the office.

Noses were plugged. Phone calls made. And we were ushered to the nurse's office to wait for our parents to bring a change of clothes.

When we were alone, I slugged Jason in the shoulder. "You should have let me throw it."

"Yeah, I should've. Then I wouldn't have to put up with you for the next two years while you're grounded. Besides, I had a motive. Now I don't have to worry about the hole in my pants."

I snickered. I couldn't help it. Maybe Jason did have hope after all.

"Clueless. I can't believe she *said* that. Out loud. In front of everyone. Right to your face!"

"I don't think she meant to be rude. Exactly."

"Yeah, it just comes naturally." I laughed, but Jason didn't join in.

Instead his shoulders drooped. "I just wish she weren't right."

I deflated. All the funny was gone. Not even Lila was laughable in the face of my best friend moving. Then it hit. I jumped to my feet. "This is about money!"

"Annie." Jason narrowed his eyes. "What are you thinking?"

"*This* is something we can fix!"

Jason stiffened. "No, it isn't. Do you even know how much houses cost?"

Mr. Gloom-and-Doom was back, but I didn't care. Ideas already swarmed my mind. I searched the room for something to write with. "I've got a plan."

3

A long list of ways to save Jason's house burned in my pocket the whole bus ride home. I tapped my foot and barely heard a word Jason said.

I was the first one off.

"Annie, wait!" Jason called, but I didn't stop.

"Come over as soon as you can." I threw the words over my shoulder. I needed to act. My ideas were *good*. We could totally save his house.

I took the stairs two at a time and dumped my backpack in the kitchen.

"Mom?"

"She's not here, dweeb. She went to a meeting." Kate glared from her homework spot. Her papers spilled halfway across our eight-person table. Sheesh. She had a desk in our room. I don't know why she didn't use it.

"Matt got in trouble *again*?" That was the only explanation. Mom spent a lot of time meeting with his teachers.

"Hey! It wasn't me this time." Matt poked his head in from the living room and stuck out his tongue.

Kate narrowed her eyes. "You're so mature."

Matt made a pig nose and snorted.

Kate pulled another textbook from her bag and slammed it down.

I jumped in before things got ugly. "So where is she, then? She's supposed to take me to soccer." She was supposed to be there, waiting for me to get home, like always. She hadn't said anything about a meeting when she brought my clothes after the lunch incident.

Kate threw down her pencil and stuffed her things into her bag. "Can I *not* get a moment of peace here? She's at the hospital, okay?" I cringed as her chair screeched against the ugly yellow linoleum. She pushed me aside on the way to our room. "*Don't* follow me."

Matt cackled like a hyena and then returned to the living room.

When the bedroom door boomed shut, I headed downstairs and pulled out the list. A meeting? My mom didn't have meetings. She took care of *us*. And why would she have a meeting at the hospital? Yeah, she used to work there, but that was forever ago. Maybe her old boss was blackmailing her. Or maybe she was secretly diagnosed with some deadly disease. Or maybe both!

As the computer finished booting, I flattened my list on our Goliath of a desk and read:

1. *Win the lottery.*
2. *Sell appendix on eBay.*
3. *Get a job (must pay $$$).*
4. *Find Jason's dad a job.*
5. *Get a loan.*

6. *Ask the bank for more time.*

7. *Beg (find a good street corner). Sing? Kazoo?*

8. *Win a radio contest.*

9. *Bingo night (with Jason's grandma?).*

10. *Bake sale.*

11. *Car wash.*

12. *Back-up plan: convince Mom and Dad to let Jason's family move into the basement.*

One was sure to work. Now I just needed to do a little research. Starting with #1. On Google's homepage, I typed "Utah lottery."

The State of Utah does not have its own lottery. I frowned. Still. Only a small setback. I could find a way around this.

I made a note on my sheet and then Googled the next idea. Jason came in dressed for soccer practice, cleats and all.

He eyed me. "You're not going in jeans are you?"

"We have half an hour. I'm fine. I've been working on our plan."

"Plan?"

"Duh. To save your house. Look." I held out the paper.

Jason studied it. "This is what you were working on in class? You're lucky Mrs. Starry didn't catch you."

"I'm a spy. I don't get caught."

His eyes move down the page. His face twitched once or twice but was otherwise unreadable.

When he finally looked up, he shrugged. "I guess one or two of these might work."

I snatched the paper away. "What do you mean, you guess? These are great ideas!"

"*Riiight*. Like the lottery."

"What's wrong with that?"

"Utah doesn't even have one. And even if we did, you'd have to be eighteen to buy a ticket."

"I know we don't —" The idea struck. "My Uncle Jim lives in Chicago. I'll ask him to help." Why hadn't I thought of that before? I scribbled a note on the page. He was a pushover of an uncle. Not even boring like most adults.

"*If* he'll help us."

"He'll help us."

"And about selling your appendix . . ."

"Yeah! I just Googled it. Look. It says right there it's legal. And I already checked on eBay. There isn't a single one for sale! No competition."

Jason brushed me aside. "Annie, no one wants your appendix." He highlighted "appendix" and typed "kidney" in its place. "This is what you probably meant. But see? It's illegal."

"What?" I squinted at the screen until I found something I liked. "Not in Iran." I took the mouse from him and clicked on a link.

We read silently. The writer of the article clearly agreed with me. Why shouldn't I be able to sell a kidney? I had two after all. And imagine the money we'd make if both of us sold one.

Jason cleared his throat. "Whatever. And getting a job? We're ten. Nobody would hire us."

"What about Hollywood? Kids act in movies all the time."

"And how are we going to get *there*?" He crossed his arms.

Here I was, trying to help him. . . . offering to donate an appendix, kidney, whatever, and all he could do was complain. Well maybe he should sell his own kidney.

"Fine. I thought you wanted to stay. My mistake." I swiveled my chair so my back was to him and counted down.

Five . . . four . . . three . . . two . . . one.

"Okay. You're right. I'm sorry."

It worked every time. I spun back around grinning. "That's all right. I know you can't help it. But what did you think *would* work?"

Jason hopped on the desk and the old metal giant groaned under his weight. "Finding my dad a job. I mean, he's looking, but in the newspaper. *Hard copy.* I bet we could find lots of stuff on the computer."

"See? We *can* do something."

I pulled a clean sheet of paper from the printer. I wrote in large print, all caps:

PLAN A: FIND JASON'S DAD A JOB.

"You know what kind of jobs to look for, right?" I tapped my pen on the paper.

Jason nodded.

"Then you can work on that one. I'll start with one of these others on the list."

Jason turned as red as strawberry jelly (my second favorite flavor and Jason's third). "Oh, but . . . I mean . . . what if my dad catches me? You should have seen him last night when my mom brought up food stamps. 'Bianca! I can handle this. I don't need your help or anyone else's!'" He mimicked his dad's voice.

Food stamps? Were they *that* poor? I thought of my Uncle Rob and Aunt Tess — the only people I knew who'd ever used them. We'd visited their dingy apartment two summers ago, and I'd gotten stuck in their ratty old couch. My mom had had to pull me out.

I kept my eyes on the list and shrugged, trying to act casual. "You can use our computer. Then he won't know unless we find something. Which we totally will."

Jason let out his breath, the red in his cheeks fading. "So if I'm doing that, what will you work on?"

I stalled. I had a couple of ideas, but I already knew Jason wouldn't approve. "Oh, you know . . ."

"No, I . . ."

"Annie!" My mom hurried into the room. I hadn't even heard her get home. She looked me over and her shoulders slumped. "Aren't you ready yet?"

I was confused. "Ready for what?"

"For soccer, Annie. What else?"

She strode across the room, and I casually leaned over my lists.

"Turn this thing off . . ." She grabbed the mouse then looked at the screen.

Uh-oh. I'd forgotten about the article.

"Kidney donation? An-nie?"

I hated it when she said my name like that. It's like her tone could pull out a confession even if I were innocent.

"Tell me this is for school. Right? Some research project?"

I glanced at Jason then back at my mom. *I'm a world-class spy. I'm a world-class spy. I can do this.* "Ye . . . no." I couldn't do it.

I know I'll be able to lie to a stranger when millions of lives are on the line, but not to my mom. "I heard part of a news show about it, and I was . . . curious." All true. True-ish, anyway.

"Annie Lynn Jenkins. Don't tell me you were thinking about . . ."

My face must have looked guilty because she got all stiff and pressed two fingers to her forehead. Never a good sign.

"We do not traffic in body parts in this household, young lady! Do you understand me?"

I nodded. Because even though I had no idea what traffic had to do with it, I was pretty sure she meant my kidney was officially off the market.

"Now go upstairs and get ready before I regret not grounding you for a month."

4

Mom was still giving me evil looks by the next morning. So when the phone rang, I had this feeling I was somehow in trouble.

I stopped chewing my Peanut Butter Rice Pops mid-bite. My spoon dripped milk onto the counter.

"Hello, Maggie," Mom spoke into the receiver. "How are you?"

Maggie? I didn't recognize the name. Maybe my instincts were off. I continued eating.

Mom glanced in my direction, smiled, and then stepped out of the kitchen.

I knew that look. Mom was making plans for me with some stranger named Maggie! I leaned forward on my bar stool, straining to hear.

"Annie would love to go. How very kind of you to invite her. But please, let me send a plate of cookies . . . I insist. And I'll speak to Bianca about Jason. I can't imagine there'd be a problem."

Was it a birthday party? Maybe Maggie was in the other fifth grade class with Mrs. Guppy. But it sounded like my mom was talking to an adult. Gah! What good was I as a super spy if I couldn't figure this out?

"Thank you again. Yes . . . You, too. Have a nice day."

Mom came back into the kitchen. She hung up the phone and leaned against the counter. "Well apparently you've made a good impression *somewhere*. That was Mrs. Schuster from across the cul-de-sac. She invited you and Jason over for cookies and milk this afternoon."

"What?! But Mo-om! I can't go to Mrs. Mean — Schuster's." I blushed at the near-fatal mistake.

"And why is that, Annie? Because you seem to have plenty of time to research illegal activities. One afternoon won't kill you."

I frantically searched for a good excuse, because not only would I be in for a miserable afternoon, but we'd have to delay Plan A. Jason was supposed to come over after my piano lessons to start the job search.

Piano lessons! Brilliant!

"I have piano lessons, Mom. Remember?" Never in a million years did I think I'd actually be grateful for the hateful things.

My mom frowned. "That's right. I forgot." She drummed her fingers on the counter, staring at nothing while I gleefully finished my cereal. I took my bowl to the sink and grabbed my backpack. I wanted to whistle, victory felt so good.

Until my mom stood up straight. "I'll just have to call your teacher and explain. Maybe we can do a make-up on Saturday. Hmm . . ." She turned her back to me, phone in one hand, list of phone numbers in the other.

"But . . ."

Mom waved me off. I glared at her back. I wanted to scream. My life was falling apart around me and there was nothing I could do.

I stomped down the stairs as loud as I could and pulled open the door. I wasn't even going to say goodbye. My mom didn't deserve it.

Halfway down the porch steps, she came flying out the front door. "You forgot your lunch, Annie." She held up an overstuffed brown paper bag. I could tell she'd remembered to pack an extra sandwich for Jason.

I debated if a hunger strike would get me out of visiting Mrs. Meany, but Society members keep their promises to each other. Grudgingly, I pulled off my backpack and stuck the lunch in.

Mom kissed me on the forehead like she did every day. "I called Jason's mom, so you're all set. The two of you will come straight here after school to pick up the cookies before going to Mrs. Schuster's. Now have a good day, Annie. I love you."

I almost cracked, almost smiled back, but a principle was at stake here. Instead I marched away.

When the bus arrived, Jason and I plopped into our seat.

"I hate visiting old people," Jason said. "I don't even like visiting my grandma, and *she* sends me money every year."

"I know," I moaned. "This totally stinks."

Jason and I were gloomy the whole morning. Every time we caught each other's eye, we'd pretend to gag.

I was so bummed that for once I didn't get sent to Mrs. Starry's "thinking corner." At lunch, we even listened to Lila's ranting without comment — until she invited us over to play her new video game. No way would I fall for that again. My hair was finally starting to look normal.

Maybe some good *would* come from this. I smiled sweetly. "Gosh. I wish we could go, Lila, but Jason and I have an appointment. Or I know! You could come with us. I bet Mrs. Meany wouldn't mind." My mom was always scolding me for not being nicer to Lila. Now I could honestly tell her I'd tried.

"Mrs. Meany's? Is that a punishment or something? No way."

The look on Lila's face would make every miserable second of the visit worth it. But I forced myself to look disappointed she wouldn't come.

"Gee, too bad. Maybe some other time." I imagined clinking my PB&J with Jason's in a toast of good fortune, since doing it for real would have looked suspicious.

The good feelings lasted right up until we were headed around the cul-de-sac. We stayed on the sidewalk because it took longer to get there that way.

"Remember, don't step on her grass," I said. "We don't want to be lectured the whole time."

"As if I'll make that mistake again. Do you think she still has my football?"

Even though it happened over a year ago, I cringed at the memory. We were practicing our spirals to show up Evan at recess the next day. But that got boring, so we upped the stakes. Super Bowl PB&JXVII.

We were down by six with a second to go. Jason Parker hiked the ball to the new quarterback phenom, Annie "The Bomb" Jenkins. I dodged a sack. Jerked free from another, then looked downfield. Parker was wide open. Crowds screaming, my long bomb sailed through the air, a perfect spiral. Parker reached, it wasn't enough. He dove for the catch and . . . Touchdown!

It'd be a great memory if Jason hadn't landed in a sliding mass on Mrs. Meany's lawn. But for the record, spiking the ball was his idea.

Not only did we suffer a lecture on the spot, Mrs. Meany confiscated Jason's football *and* called both our moms that night.

Ugh.

But that was a whole year ago. For Jason's sake, I played it cool. "I'm sure she's yelled at so many kids she can't keep them straight. I wouldn't worry about it. I mean, she wouldn't have invited us over just to yell at us some more. Would she?"

"Um . . ."

"Of course she wouldn't." I marched up the driveway past the perfectly trimmed grass. I resisted the urge to touch the pansies in the flowerbed along the porch. And though the garden gnome practically called my name, I didn't splash any water from the basin it held. I gripped the plate with two hands and nodded at the old-fashioned knocker on the door.

"You'll have to do it."

Jason glared at me as he passed. He tapped it three times and then scooted behind me. The coward.

"Why do you think she put a bench around that tree?" Balancing the cookies with one hand, I pointed to the white, metal bench that circled a slender tree in her yard. "I mean, if she's so crabby about people walking on her grass, what's the point?"

"I just think it looks nice." Mrs. Schuster stood in the doorway.

I whirled around and the plate of cookies flipped out of my hand. I looked from Mrs. Meany to the crumbled cookies. "I didn't mean that, honest, I was just . . ." A quick glance at Jason told me he'd be no help. He looked like a wax dummy.

Not knowing what else to do, I scooped up the baggie and swished the crumbs back onto the plate. I held it out. Maybe I'd get lucky and she'd decide not to go through with this. "My mom made these."

Mrs. Schuster shook her head then stepped aside. "Please, come in. And thank you for coming to share some . . . er . . . crumbs with a crabby old lady."

"Thank you, Mrs. Mean—" My face burned. I stared at her in alarm. "I mean, Mrs. Schuster."

Jason smacked his forehead with his palm.

But to my surprise, Mrs. Schuster laughed. "You'd better come in before that mouth of yours gets you into real trouble. Lucky for you, I haven't drunk my dose of sour prune juice today."

I hesitated. Was she for real? From anyone else, I'd know they were joking, but sour prune juice would explain a lot.

Jason nudged me. "Come on. Let's get this over with."

Just inside was a for-show-only sitting room with perfectly straight vacuum lines. Mrs. Schuster ushered us down a picture-clad hallway and into the kitchen. It was as perfect as her yard and her sitting room. Not a dish out of place. She motioned toward a square table surrounded by chairs just off the kitchen. "Go ahead and sit. I'll find some bowls for these crumbs . . . and maybe some spoons." She winked like it was some big joke. "And I'll get you both a tall glass of that prune juice I mentioned."

My mouth dropped open. She *was* serious!

Mrs. Schuster wheezed a laugh. "I'm kidding. My drink of choice is milk. Sound okay?"

"D-do you need help?" Jason asked.

Mrs. Schuster waved him off. "When I'm in a wheelchair, I still won't let my guests help. Now get on with you."

After what seemed like forever, the three of us sat facing each other with bowls of cookie clumps and tall glasses of milk. At first I was impressed she gave us glass glasses, until I realized she didn't own anything else.

We ate in silence for a good five minutes. Seriously, I could hear crickets. Still, the crumbs melted in my mouth. My mom's cookies are good no matter how *or* where you serve them.

Finally, Mrs. Shuster spoke. "Your mother's cookies are legend in these parts. Be sure to thank her for me. Actually, you should really thank her for yourselves. My cookies are legend in these parts, too. But not in a positive light."

Jason and I shared a look.

I stuffed a heaping spoonful of crumbs in my mouth so I wouldn't have to say anything.

She cleared her throat. "So. You're probably wondering why I invited you two over, given our . . . rocky history. Now let's be honest. I know your parents made you come. Otherwise there's no way in . . . well, I doubt you two would spend a Friday afternoon with an old crab like me."

I nearly spewed crumbs across the table. Jason spit a mouthful of milk back in his glass and started trying to cough up a lung.

Though I was shocked to my toes, I kind of started to like her. I mean the lady had spunk. "I don't think you're a crab, Mrs. Schuster," I lied.

"I know all about my reputation in the neighborhood, young lady. And I earned every bit of it. I was awfully crabby, but I've decided to change. That's why I invited you over. But first, a peace offering." She walked around the table to a cedar chest in the corner and pulled out a football. "Here you are, young man." Mrs. Schuster handed it to Jason. "I suppose it's high time I returned your property."

Jason beamed. "Thanks!"

Mrs. Schuster sat. "I was sulking, you know."

I'd never heard an adult admit to sulking before. Another point in her favor.

"A couple years back, my son and I had a fight . . . well, we can call it a feisty disagreement. That sounds so much better. One little heart attack, and he insisted I move to a retirement home. At sixty, imagine! He drew up papers and everything assuming I'd just go along, the idiot."

Jason kicked me under the table and we shared a grin. She'd said *idiot*!

"And then, to make sure I stayed good and angry, he put me on the mailing lists of every retirement home in a fifty-mile radius. But look at me . . . blabbering on." Mrs. Schuster sniffed. "The point is I want to change my crabby ways. So come on. Let me show you something."

We followed her down a second hallway leading toward the bedrooms. She grabbed a hooked metal stick leaning against the wall and pulled a rope down from the ceiling. "You look like a strapping lad. Pull this." She handed the rope to Jason, who had to drop his whole weight on it before anything would budge.

To my delight, a section of the ceiling dropped down to form stairs. "A hidden room!" I'd only ever seen these in movies. The old lady was gaining my esteem fast.

Mrs. Schuster chuckled. "Not really a secret room. That rope would give it away pretty quickly, but it is a fun contraption, isn't it? Now up we go."

The attic was filled with boxes and all sorts of old-looking things: an old-fashioned mannequin wore a large hat loaded with feathers; an empty birdcage hung from a hook in one of the beams; an ugly green leather chair sat against one wall. But most surprising was how messy it was. Dust caked the floor and everything else, though a path had been cleared toward a chest in the corner.

I caught my breath. A pirate's chest! I could tell by the skull-shaped keyhole. Being the only dust-less item in the room, I guessed this was what Mrs. Schuster had brought us to see. Jason and I crossed the room in less than a second, running our fingers along the bone engravings on the black trim.

"I finally decided to tackle the skeletons here in the attic when I came across it."

"Skeletons?" Jason jumped back from the chest.

Mrs. Schuster wheezed a laugh. "It's an expression, dear boy. It means facing your past. When my Ned died, my son helped me move his things up here. I couldn't bear to look at any of it. It just made me too sad. I haven't touched it since, but that was over twenty years ago. I figured it was high time I faced my past."

Wow. I didn't know she'd been a widow for so long. I started to feel a little bad for calling her Mrs. Meany all those years.

Mrs. Schuster pulled an oversized skeleton key from her pocket and handed it to Jason. "Go on. Open it."

"Was this your husband's?" I asked.

"Of course it isn't. I haven't gotten up the guts to look through his stuff yet. This belonged to my great-great-grandmother, Cap'n Black Marge. She was a pirate."

Jason stuck the key in the keyhole, and I shivered when it clicked into place. What if this was a real, live treasure chest? Mrs. Schuster had said it once belonged to a pirate. What if we opened it to find gold and jewels just like in the movies? I'd been praying for a miracle since I saw that For Sale sign, and maybe this was it! I mean, surely Mrs. Schuster would share since she'd invited us to see it.

The hinges screeched as he pushed open the lid, and my excitement fizzled.

Clothes. Nothing but clothes.

"Cool!" Jason said. "Pirate clothes."

I guess he hadn't been expecting gold.

"Go on, see what there is. I thought you might enjoy playing dress-up with these. In fact, the whole trunk is for you two. I hope you don't mind sharing." She settled herself in the old green chair.

I wanted to tell her that dress-up was for babies, but Jason beat me to the punch.

"We get to keep this? Trunk and all?" Jason grinned so wide I thought his face would burst.

Or not. Apparently he hadn't gotten there yet. That place where he realizes that we can't possibly share the chest because he'll be moving to California if we don't do something about it — and soon.

Both Mrs. Schuster and Jason looked so excited, I put on a front, but my heart was with the list of plans I'd been making back home.

Jason pulled out a silky purple cloth and shook it open. The neck opened in a wide V-shape, and the sleeves hung long with scads of extra material at the ends.

"It's an old-fashioned tunic." Mrs. Schuster explained. "The men used to wear those if you can believe it."

I pulled at some crimson velvet that turned out to be a vest with gold, skull-shaped buttons. I held it up to me, but it was several sizes too big.

Jason pulled out a brown leather eye patch with a pearl sewn in the center. He tried it on.

"Aaaargh. Walk the plank, me hearties," Jason growled. He flipped the eye patch back up. "I think I just decided what I want to be for Halloween this year."

I could only stare at Jason. He could be gone by then. This chest was turning into one big heap of gloom.

I concentrated on the items in the chest: a royal blue jacket with gold trimming; thigh-high boots with large silver buckles; an off-white, puffed-sleeve tunic made of damask (or so Mrs. Schuster claimed); a boatload of bracelets and chain necklaces; a couple pairs of funny-looking trousers with square fronts that buttoned up on either side; silk scarves; and a tri-cornered hat with a fluffy green feather.

Some of the stuff could make for awesome burial ceremonies. Instead of time-outs we could institute a speaking-hat. Or we could add a fancy inspection jacket to show how important it was. I made a mental note to suggest this at our next PB&J Society meeting.

At the very bottom of the chest lay a rolled-up scroll of brown, crusting paper. I held it up for the others to see. "This must be the treasure map."

I'd been joking, but Mrs. Schuster's eyes nearly popped out of her head. "That was in there? Open it. Hurry."

I slipped off the rusty iron ring, then spread the paper smooth on the floor. Jason and Mrs. Schuster crowded around.

"It *is* a map! And look, there's an X, just like in the movies."

Mrs. Schuster rubbed her neck, which was splotchy with excitement. "I grew up on stories of Black Marge's hidden treasure, but I never thought it could be true."

"Treasure? *Real* treasure?" Now she was speaking my language.

"Hey! This looks like our neighborhood," Jason said. He pointed to the thick blue wavy lines that ran along the top. "That would be the canal, and here's the ditch." He moved his finger along the thin blue off-shoot that trailed down the far side of the page. Next he pinched his fingers by the map legend at the bottom, then measured a distance from the canal. "There." He tapped a spot by the ditch. "According to the legend, your house is here."

Right next to the X.

I had long since stopped believing in fairy tales, but pirates had really existed. What if this was real? I mean, isn't this how it always worked in stories? Just when it all seemed hopeless, a fairy appeared, a treasure was discovered, or a prince came to save the day. That was just what I needed.

I looked at Jason and could tell he was thinking the same thing. A lost treasure could save his house.

"Now I know what you're probably thinking," Mrs. Schuster said, "and you can just get that thought right out of your heads."

My heart sank. Of course she was going to claim this map as hers. She may want to change, but my mom's always telling me that change doesn't happen overnight. The Mrs. Meany I knew would never give up a real treasure map.

"This map absolutely belongs to you. I gave you that chest and everything in it, including the map."

My heart nearly leapt out of my chest.

"But I have a proposal. I'll tell you everything I know about that treasure and Black Marge if you'll come visit me . . . keep me updated on your search." She leaned forward. "You are going to search for Cap'n Black Marge's treasure, aren't you?"

Jason didn't say anything, but I was already up and shaking her hand on the deal. "Of course we are!"

5

It wasn't a minute after shaking hands with Mrs. Schuster that an alarm went off somewhere downstairs. Mrs. Schuster rolled her eyes.

"Stupid buzzard," she said. "I'm afraid we'll have to call it a day. I'll ask one of your fathers to come get this old trunk out of my house."

I was actually disappointed to leave before hearing more about Black Marge.

"Don't forget, we agreed!" Mrs. Schuster called from the doorway.

"You, too!" I grinned. A lost treasure! How could this not be fate? We would find it, and Jason would get to stay. No selling of kidneys necessary.

"It's pizza night. Think your mom'll let you eat over? Then we can study this map for clues." I gripped the scroll, wishing I could rip it open right there. But my fine-tuned spy skills would never let me do something so foolish. We couldn't risk letting enemy eyes get a peek at this.

"I'll call from your house, but she'll say yes." Jason flipped his football in the air and caught it. "Maybe we can even look for some jobs for my dad."

"Good idea. A good spy always has a backup plan."

Jason stopped. "Annie. Looking for jobs is Plan A, not the backup. Remember? Besides, you don't really believe there's a treasure, do you?"

"So Mr. Yay-we-get-clothes-for-dress-up is too old to believe in treasure?" I threw the words over my shoulder, not stopping.

Jason ran to catch up like I knew he would. His chipmunk cheeks were red. "I was being polite. Besides, Halloween is coming up. It *would* be cool to be a pirate for Halloween. Did you see that eye patch?"

"You won't even be here on Halloween if we don't find that treasure. And don't change the subject." I was annoyed. "Mrs. Schuster's eyes practically bugged out of her head when she saw this map. It has to be real."

"We live in Utah, Annie. That's like thousands of miles from the ocean. Even if Black Marge *did* exist, how in the world did she end up here? Especially with a heavy treasure. It's not like they had cars. They probably didn't even have trains back then. It just doesn't make sense."

"Why does everything have to make sense?" I asked. I wanted to slap him across the face to knock some sense into him. "What doesn't make sense is that you have to move because of stupid money. What if there *is* a treasure and we don't find it because you won't even look?"

Jason didn't say anything as we crossed my front yard. When I plopped onto the top porch step, he cleared his throat. "Finding my dad a job is a better plan. Mrs. Schuster is probably lying."

"Why would she lie to us?"

Jason looked away. "Adults lie all the time."

I knew he meant his dad. All summer long, Mr. Parker had backed out on every plan they'd made — fishing, hiking, camping. Jason didn't talk about it, but best friends know.

"But why? Why would Mrs. Schuster invite us over special to lie to us?" I plucked a dandelion from the grass and with a puff, sent the seeds dancing through the air.

"Why would she lie?" Jason asked. "A better question is why would she suddenly decide to give a family heirloom to two kids she doesn't even like?"

I'd opened my mouth to answer when inspiration struck. I didn't need to convince Jason about the *treasure*. He just needed to help me search.

I tapped my mouth, pretending to think about what he said. "Hmm, maybe you're right. What we have here is a bona fide mystery. Even if you don't believe in the treasure, don't you want answers?"

Jason picked at a scab on his elbow, pretending not to care. "I don't know. It doesn't really matter."

"A real mystery, Jason. Plopped in our laps. You're not seriously going to ignore it, are you?"

Jason scuffed his foot on the walkway. I had him. "It would be our first real case," he said softly.

"Exactly! If we can't earn the money, don't you want to go out with a bang? We can solve this thing."

"Will we still look for jobs for my dad?"

"Plan A, remember? Treasure will be Plan B, and I've got some ideas for C and D."

His eyes narrowed. "You still think the treasure's real, don't you?"

"Geez, you act like it would be a bad thing if we actually found it."

Jason sighed. "Fine. What do we have to do?"

"Look for the treasure. Report to Mrs. Schuster. Just like we agreed. Are you in?" I held out my hand. "Peanut butter."

Jason rubbed the back of his neck, then sighed. "Jelly." He gripped my hand and we clapped our other hands over the top and bottom of them to make a sandwich.

One final shake, and according to Society rules the pact was made. There was no going back after the handshake.

We ran inside and up to the kitchen. No one was there.

"Mom! Can Jason eat over?" I yelled.

She answered from the laundry room downstairs. "As long as it's okay with his mom!"

I grinned at Jason and grabbed the phone just as it rang. I fumbled the thing, barely catching it before it hit the floor.

"Nice show." Jason looked like the Cheshire Cat.

Ignoring him, I punched the talk button. "Hello?"

"Is Mrs. Jenkins available, please?"

Drat. I should have looked at the caller ID. Obviously a telemarketer. Mom hated it when we answered those. "May I ask who's calling?"

"This is Mr. Archer from the Regional Hospital. I'm . . ."

I didn't hear the rest because my mom came bounding up the stairs like a crazy person, balancing a full laundry basket on her hip. "Is that for me? Here! Give me the phone!" She dropped the basket and yanked the phone from my hand. "Hello?"

Jason and I stared. I'd never seen my mom like this.

"Oh, yes! Mr. Archer. So nice to hear from you." She frowned when she caught us staring. "I'm sorry, can you hold for just a minute? . . . Thank you." She covered the mouthpiece. "You two should be outside. It's a beautiful day. I'll let you know when the pizza gets here. You both like pepperoni, right?"

"But we haven't called Jason's mom yet."

"I'll take care of it when I'm done here. Now scoot."

"Can I at least get something from my room?"

"One thing, Annie. But I'd better not catch you dawdling." She uncovered the mouthpiece and headed for her room. "Sorry about that. Please, go ahead." The door slammed shut and I couldn't hear anything else. I debated using the Spy Bud 2000, but I was still on thin ice from the kidney incident.

"That was weird," Jason said.

"For real. Talk about a mystery."

Still holding the map, I grabbed my spy notepad and a pen and we headed out back. We scooted two white plastic deck chairs to the table and made a list of everything we remembered from our visit with Mrs. Schuster.

Mrs. Schuster invited us for milk and cookies.

She gave Jason back his football.

She claims she wants to change — be less crabby.

"And don't forget what she said about her family," Jason added.

"She had a husband?"

"Who died twenty years ago. And she has a son."

"Who she's mad at." I still couldn't believe she'd called him an idiot.

Husband died twenty years ago.

Son she's mad at.

Had a heart attack a couple years ago.

Claims to have a great-great-grandmother named Captain Black Marge.

Mysterious alarm went off at 4:30 p.m.

Gave us a pirate's chest full of pirate's clothes and a "treasure map."

We argued about the quotes around it, but I finally gave in. If that kept Jason interested, whatever. He could think what he wanted as long as he helped me look for the treasure.

Promised to help us if we report back to her on our search.

Jason read through the clues. "I don't know, Annie. It kind of just sounds like she's lonely."

I frowned, afraid he was right. But it couldn't be that easy. "But why us?" I asked. "And why now? If she's just lonely, she could talk to other old people — like my mom or something. Wouldn't that be better than inviting over a couple of kids who ruined her lawn?"

Jason sat up straighter. "You're right! Write that down."

After I added it, we pulled out the map.

We studied every square inch of that thing, but the only hint we could find about where the treasure might be buried was the actual X.

"Well I bet the treasure's buried by the ditch. Pirates always bury their treasure near water."

Jason squinted at the map and did some more finger measurements. "I don't know. We don't have much to go on here. And now that I think about it, was the canal even built back then? I doubt the irrigation ditches are that old."

"Of course they are. Don't you remember your Utah history from last year? The canals and ditches were like the first thing the pioneers built. Even before houses."

Jason gave me a dirty look. He was usually the one who reminded me of stuff we were supposed to have learned.

"Now come on. We have nothing to lose. We search for an X somewhere along the ditch, then report back to Mrs. Schuster for more info. Tomorrow before our soccer game. Besides, we haven't explored the African jungle in ages."

"Fine."

We grabbed our ditch shoes from below the deck and stuffed my spy notepad and the map in our regular shoes.

I was nervous about leaving the map. "Maybe you should use your shirt to cover it," I told Jason.

He backed away. "Are you crazy? I'm not taking my shirt off in front of you."

I rolled my eyes. "We're going to the ditch. That's practically like going swimming. You never have a problem taking your shirt off at the pool."

Jason's eyes narrowed. "The ditch is like three inches deep. Nothing like going to the pool. You seem awful anxious for me to take my shirt off."

I couldn't help it. My cheeks flamed. "I'm not! I wanted to protect the map, but forget it. If it gets stolen and someone else finds the treasure, don't blame me."

We stood there glaring for a minute until I bolted. "Beat you there!"

"Cheater!" Jason wasn't far behind. His pounding footsteps were getting closer.

I made it to the end of the yard a millisecond before him and splashed water in his direction. "I win!"

He kicked water back at me. "Only because you cheated."

Not that I'd admit it to him, but he was definitely faster than me. It was rather disturbing.

I pretended I didn't hear him and headed to the forest gateway.

Most yards were fenced off from the irrigation ditch, so weeds and willowy trees grew high around it. But not mine. Dad planted grass right up to the edge so we could play in the water when it was turned on through the summer. With no fence to keep us out, the willowy archway into the rest of the ditch was like a magical door.

Before going in, I gasped. "Did you see that?" I pointed at the gateway. "Hurry! It's a leopard."

I sprinted into the jungle with Jason close behind.

"It's about to eat that penguin!" Jason hid behind a sprawling weed.

"There are no penguins in *Africa*." I crouched next to him.

"Why not?" Jason shrugged. "It's all pretend anyway, so why not mix it up?"

I shook my head. "That's like having a shark fly. There are *rules*, you know."

"That's the stupidest thing I've ever heard."

"You could probably get away with a koala," I suggested. "See the one in that tree?"

"Koalas live in Australia," Jason said.

"But it's hot in Australia, like it is in Africa, so it's okay."

Jason glared for another second, then a grin crept up his face. "Uh-oh. The koala just sprung a trap. I hear the hunters coming."

"Hey! Leave my koala alone." I'd simply free the koala if I hadn't been down this road before. Jason would keep coming up with rotten tricks till I gave in. Not today. There would be no penguins in Africa. I spun around and marched farther into the jungle.

"Aren't hunters allowed in the rules?" Jason called.

I glanced back. Jason threw back his head and laughed evilly. "Bwah, hah, hah!"

Splashing as much as I could, I stomped farther into the forest. I hadn't gone far when Jason called out.

"Oh my gosh! Annie, come see this!"

"I'm not falling for it." I stuck my nose in the air.

"Serious, Annie. It's an X!"

One look and I knew he wasn't joking. I raced back, grabbing a stick on the way. Jason hefted a rock where I could clearly see the rough scrapings of a white X-mark. It looked familiar. I'd probably seen it dozens of times on other explorations without realizing what it was.

"Use this." I pushed the stick at him, and Jason launched into digging.

I held my breath and imagined finding a second chest to match the one Mrs. Schuster had given us — only this one filled with gold. I saw the awe in my parent's eyes. The respect on Mr. Parker's face. Mrs. Parker's tears of gratitude when we paid off the house. A stray thought of an iPhone wiggled in — make that matching iPhones for Jason and me. I couldn't help grinning.

The stick clanged against something and Jason threw it away to dig with his hands.

I saw a flash of silver. I wanted to dance. Celebrate. It was all I could do not to jump with excitement.

Jason pulled the object free. He dipped it in the ditch to wash off the dirt, then held it up.

My joy crashed into the mud. "My Miss Piggy alarm clock. I forgot about that." That's why the X looked so familiar. Jason and I scratched it on that rock with my dad's best screwdriver forever ago. Man was he mad.

Jason's lips quivered. I was afraid he might cry until he snorted a laugh. He clutched his stomach. He laughed so hard, he shook.

I wanted to be mad. That clock marked a tragic moment in my life. My five-year-old self had been deeply scarred. A chuckle escaped.

Jason dropped to his knees. Gasping for breath, he held up the clock and tried to speak. "I can't . . ." And he burst into another fit. Tears streamed down his face.

Jason looked foolish, wheezing and pointing. I snickered then laughed harder. Soon I was wiping away my own tears.

When we finally managed to stop, Jason shook his head. "I still can't believe your mom actually *said* you were eating Miss Piggy." He handed me the clock — a.k.a. the pig sacrifice.

I flicked one of the rusting silver bells on top, but it didn't ring. From behind the scratched glass facing, Miss Piggy smiled broadly in her purple shimmery dress. Her arms still marked the exact moment my mom had shattered my innocence: the short arm pointed to the six and the long arm to the three.

"I still don't like pork chops."

Jason took a deep breath, wiped the last tears from his eyes, and stood. "Let's go see if that pizza's here yet. I'm starving."

We trudged back to my house. Though the dig had been a bust, I wasn't about to give up. Cap'n Black Marge's treasure could fix everything.

6

After I'd eaten three slices of pizza and Jason five, we headed to the computer. Matt was still chowing down on his, like, seventh piece, and Kate had shut herself away in our room, talking to her friend, Emma, on the phone.

"Do you know where to search?" I asked.

Jason shrugged. "That's what Google is for."

As soon as the computer had booted, he cracked his fingers and began the search. He skipped over the Department of Workforce site, certain his dad had visited them a few weeks ago in person. After perusing several links, he settled on a local TV station and pages of jobs popped up.

I flipped on the radio and waited through two songs while Jason scrolled through the lists.

"Find anything?" I finally asked.

Jason didn't look away from the screen. "Hmm. Not yet."

I sighed. "Why don't we just print the whole list off and let your dad choose?" I punched the power button on the printer.

Jason rolled his eyes and pointed at the screen. "Look. Engineering, engineering, engineering. Manufacturing,

IT, mechanical services. He doesn't qualify for these. We have to find the good ones and print those off."

I crossed my arms. Jason had no imagination. Stuck in his little box of logic. "But isn't that the point? If he could find a job doing what he used to do, he'd already be working, right? So we need to find him a new one. Preferably one that makes lots of money."

I scanned the list. "Here's one. Director of Operations. Didn't your dad run his own business before? He'd be great at that, and it probably makes boatloads of money."

Jason clicked on it. "It's for a funeral home, Annie. Plus it says right there you need a Bachelor's plus ten years experience."

"Well doesn't he have that? He's old enough."

Jason's nostrils flared, but he didn't take his eyes off the screen. "Nope."

"Oh." I scanned the list again. "What about that one? 'Shop Assistant (Entry Level).' I mean, I know your mom does the shopping usually, but I bet your dad has learned a few things from her. Plus it's entry level, so they won't expect him to have experience!"

Jason smacked his forehead. "*Shop* assistant, not shopping. That means he'd work at a car place." He clicked on the job. "See?"

"Oh." I read through the job description. There were hardly any requirements for this one, and I still thought his dad could do it until the part where it said, "must have good attitude." He'd been struggling with that one lately.

"Look, why don't you just let me search on my own for a minute. I know what I'm looking for."

"Fine." I flopped onto the old orange and white barn-print couch. Ugliest couch ever. But at least it gave me something to do. I focused on finding the hidden cats and decided I could do it by the end of the current song on the radio.

Except I overestimated how much of the song was left. The deejay was blabbing on about some hair growth product and I was about to change it until I heard the magic words.

"*Right now! Caller twenty-two wins a thousand dollars of cold, hard cash. 4-8-1, 5-8-1, or 6-8-1-CASH. That's 4-8-1, 5-8-1, or 6-8-1-2-2-7-4. Caller twenty-two. Good luck!*"

I bolted to the phone and dialed the number, but when I held it to my ear, all I got was Kate screaming at me.

"Hey! I'm on the phone! Hang it up. Now!"

"This is urgent! I'll only be two minutes and you can call Emma right back. Please!"

The deejay on the radio was answering the calls live. "*Hello! You're caller number seven, try again.*"

"No way, squirt. I had it first."

"Please! With sugar on top and extra cherries."

"I hate cherries. Now hang up before I make you."

"*Too bad! You're caller number eleven, keep trying.*"

Big sisters were so overrated. Well, two could play at that game. "If you don't let me make my call, I'm telling Emma about your last journal entry where you . . ."

58

"Okay! Okay. I'm hanging up, but you have two minutes. Got that?"

Emma was yelling over Kate, making it hard to hear. "Wait! What journal entry?!"

"Hello! You're caller number sixteen, try again."

Then it all went silent. I hung up, my heart pounding, and dialed again as soon as I heard the dial tone. I only had seconds.

Jason glanced at me from the computer and shook his head. Pessimist.

I held my breath, and yes! The phone was ringing! My heart pounded as I waited.

Two rings. Three.

"Congratulations! You're caller number twenty-two! You've just won a thousand dollars!"

I screamed. "Oh my gosh! I won! I won!"

"You won?!" Jason jumped up from the computer and danced with me.

"And who do we have on the phone tonight?"

I was so excited, I couldn't remember. "Um . . . My name? Uh, it's Annie. My name's Annie."

"Well, Annie . . . you sound kind of young. How old are you, sweetheart?"

"I'm ten! And I can't believe I won!"

Jason stopped dancing when I said my age. He stared at me, then smacked his forehead.

"What?" I mouthed.

But the deejay answered my question.

"Oh, no. I'm sorry, sweetie, but you have to be eighteen to win. Looks like our winner tonight will be caller twenty-three. Let's go back to the phones."

The line went dead. He didn't even say goodbye.

Jason and I stood there in silence until Kate exploded into the room.

She grabbed the phone from my hand, then got in my face. "And just so we're clear. You are so dead for reading my journal."

She spun around and stomped back upstairs.

Great. Not only did I not get the money, now I'd be fearing for my life until Kate exacted revenge.

"So." Jason smiled. "On the bright side, I found some jobs that could work. Can I print them off?"

7

"Are you sure she'll be awake this early?" Jason hung back at the end of Mrs. Schuster's driveway.

I spun around, hands on my hips. "Don't be such a baby! All old people get up early because of the Great Depression. Or something. Seven o'clock is late to them." Gripping the rolled-up map, I marched straight to the door and knocked.

Another minute, another knock. I put my ear to the door, hoping to hear something. Anything. Finally a shuffling sound approached.

I smiled big waiting for Mrs. Schuster to answer.

"Don't you people know what time it is?!" The door slammed open, and I shrieked. I couldn't help it.

Mrs. Schuster looked like an alien — green goo all over her face, a plastic hair net, and a flapping bathrobe. I tried to look away, but the horrific sight held me like a deer in headlights. Ewww! Sure, people looked like this on TV and it was funny *then*. In person, not so much.

"Annie! Jason!" Mrs. Schuster clutched at her bathrobe and opened the screen door. "What in Larry's name are you doing here so early on a Saturday?"

"Don't you get up at five?" I prepared to flee.

"Where did you get a fool notion like that? Come on, come on." She ushered us to the kitchen and waved toward the table "I guess you'll be wanting breakfast now, too."

"Oh, no. I had Fruity Discs before I came. Jason, too. Right?" I smacked him with my elbow hoping he'd take the hint.

"Oh. Right." He spoke in monotone.

That boy needed to work on his acting. Pitiful.

"Fruity Discs do *not* count. You give me a minute to take care of this," she motioned toward her face, "then I'll get us breakfast."

The "minute" felt like hours. We squirmed in our seats at the table waiting for Mrs. Schuster. I stared at the clock as it tick-tocked our Saturday away.

Jason tapped at the table, a frown etched on his face. Waiting was dull, but not that horrible. Then my stomach dropped. What if his house had sold!

I tried to act casual. "What's wrong? You look like someone smushed your peanut butter and jelly sandwich on purpose."

Jason sighed and shook his head. "I gave the list of jobs to my dad last night."

I could breathe again. "Yeah? Is he going to apply for any of them? Was he super grateful?"

Jason snorted. "Well, he was *super* something. Just not grateful. He ripped up the pages and said he didn't need a child to find him a job. Said he could do it on his own."

"What?! That's the stupidest thing I ever heard."

Jason raised his eyebrows but didn't say anything.

I crossed my arms. "If he doesn't need our help, then why doesn't he have a job already? Your dad should be asking for our help. But no, we have to sneak behind his back because of his stubborn . . ."

One look at Jason and I cut my rant short. He stared at the floor like he wished it would swallow him.

I thought of that thousand dollars the radio station cheated me out of. His dad would have taken that.

"Well, whatever." I pulled open the map to distract myself. Besides, with Plan A out the window (or in the garbage can, whatever), Plan B took top priority.

"Maybe we can find a clue while we wait," I suggested.

Jason sighed. "Annie, it's not real. I don't know why you bother."

"Just because your dad got mad at you doesn't mean we can't help."

He glared at me. "The map's not real."

I shifted so my back was toward him. "Fine. I'll find the clue."

He scooted closer. "Look at it. If that paper were over a hundred years old, it'd be crumbling and fragile."

"It is crumbling. See the edges?"

He fingered the paper. "But the rest of it isn't. The edges just look burned to me."

I pulled away from him. "You'd doubt your own name if it weren't written on your underwear."

He didn't say anything. Just scooted his chair back and glared at nothing.

I ignored him. He's the one who had attacked first. I'd been defending myself. Besides, he was wrong about the map. I went back to studying, but I couldn't focus. All I could see was the sturdy paper it was written on.

What if he was right? I glanced at him, hoping to catch his eye, but he didn't move.

No. It had to be real. I shook my head to clear it of Jason's poisonous doubts. Because why would Mrs. Schuster lie to us?

We waited the next twenty minutes in uncomfortable silence until Mrs. Schuster poked her head in from the kitchen. The green goo was gone along with the hair net. "Now how do you like your eggs?"

Jason came out of his trance. He still wouldn't look at me. "Over-hard. And can I have three, please?"

"Now that's what I like to see. A boy with an appetite. How about four?"

Jason looked like he'd been chosen first in kickball. Mrs. Schuster headed toward the kitchen.

I cleared my throat. "I like mine the same way."

"Of course you do! You two aren't best friends for nothing, are you?" She winked and hurried into the kitchen, causing a flurry of clinks and clanks.

It wasn't long before the smell of fried eggs had us both drooling.

But the uncomfortable silence was back.

Finally, Jason spoke. "Look." He pointed at the family pictures on the wall. "Maybe we can find some clues there."

Did that mean he forgave me for the underwear comment? I dared a smile in his direction, and he eventually returned it.

"Great idea," I said.

At eye-level, an old black-and-white showed a boy on a Red Rocket trike. Another picture with a young-looking Mrs. Schuster and her husband had been painted. Not quite a photo, not quite a painting. A series of family shots showed the gradually aging Schusters. I giggled at the wide collars and funny hair-dos.

By far, my favorite was the metal-framed picture of the teenage son in a football uniform. Mr. Schuster had his arm around him. The father looked so happy. You could almost feel it coming from the photo. Without thinking, I reached out to touch it.

"Scott looked handsome in his uniform . . . his father was proud."

I yanked my hand back and Jason whirled around.

Happiness softened Mrs. Schuster's face for a moment. Then it was gone. Her whole body seemed to droop. "That was years before he became the idiot he is today. Taken not long before my Ned died. Back in ninety-five."

"Your husband?" I asked.

Mrs. Schuster nodded. She set three food-filled plates on the table. "I'll pour us some milk, and we can eat."

We slipped back to our places and stared at our over-hard eggs and toast. Jason clapped his hands over his stomach when it growled like a starving wolf.

Mrs. Schuster returned with three large glasses of milk. "Well, go on! Those eggs aren't getting any warmer." She handed us each a glass, then sat down before placing hers next to a little cup of pills.

"Eat!" She waved us on, then plunked a slice of toast into her runny yoke.

I cut into my eggs, but I couldn't stop the question that slipped out. "Are you sick?" I peeked at Jason and could tell he was mentally adding the pills to the list.

Mrs. Schuster picked up the little cup and rattled it. "You mean these? These are my doctor's idea of a practical joke. How many pills can an old lady take at a time without choking?" She emptied the contents into her mouth and with a big swig of milk, swallowed them. "We're up to seven, and I still have the upper hand."

I laughed. She even made taking pills fun. My admiration grew. How could she possibly be lying about the treasure? She couldn't.

Mrs. Schuster finished her second wedge of toast before breaking the silence. She nodded at the scroll by my plate. "Have you done any searching? Are you ready to hear more?"

I popped in my last bite of egg, but Jason was already finished. He told her about the X and the Miss Piggy alarm clock. I was a little irked. He could have left *that* out.

And then he finished up with his doubts about the age of the canal and ditch.

"We looked at the map for any clues, but we couldn't find anything." I pushed my plate aside and spread the map on the table. "Are we missing something?"

Mrs. Schuster leaned forward and studied it for what felt like hours. I slumped in my chair when she shook her head. "I'm afraid I don't see anything either. Though that doesn't rule out any hidden clues on the map. Cap'n Black Marge *was* a master of deception."

Hidden clues! Why didn't I think of that? A memory of invisible ink joggled in my brain. I couldn't wait to test my theory when we got back to my house.

"Maybe if you told us more about Cap'n Black Marge, that'd give us a hint where to look." Jason cast a look in my direction. He wanted to catch her in a lie. He just couldn't accept the truth. Well, two could play at that game.

"How did Black Marge end up in Utah?" I asked.

Mrs. Schuster chuckled. "Well, the story goes that after being the terror of the seven seas for twenty years, Cap'n Black Marge got the urge to settle down and have kids. First, she debated kidnapping a couple of babies, but the Cap'n was smart. Smart enough to know that she didn't want to end up with just any children.

"So one May, in the middle of the night, when they were just off the coast of California, she packed her bags and the chest I gave you and slipped away on a dinghy. Of course, the crew never heard from her again."

"So how'd she get *here*?" I glanced at the clock. 8:15. We had time. Our soccer game didn't start till nine.

Mrs. Schuster cleared her throat. "Well, after leaving her crew, Black Marge decided she'd had enough of the seas, so she hired a wagon and headed east. They say she was so taken with the mountains, and relieved to find the smell of salt air, she decided to stay right here."

I threw Jason a smug look. Perfectly logical.

Mrs. Schuster stood and collected our plates. "Well. My Ned always washed his breakfast down with a cup of coffee. Perhaps you two would like hot cocoa instead?"

We both nodded (Jason a little overenthusiastically), and she disappeared into the kitchen again.

"See?" I whispered.

He crossed his arms. "Anyone can make up a story. I want details. Evidence."

I rolled my eyes, and neither of us spoke again until she came back in with three steaming mugs on a tray.

"Sorry that took so long." She placed a hot chocolate and spoon before each of us. "My hands just don't work like they used to."

Jason picked up his mug and blew steam from the top all casual-like. "That's okay. But could you tell us more about Cap'n Black Marge? Like what'd she do when she got here? Did she keep pirating?"

Mrs. Schuster shook her head. "Nope. She gave it all up, if you can believe it. First she hid her loot, then she managed to secure a job at the local feed and seed.

Orneriest clerk there ever was, but by golly she was good at getting people to buy stuff they didn't need. Intimidated them all . . . right up until Edward Smith came to town. He refused to buy those gigantic belt buckles he didn't need, and he wouldn't even look twice at the lima beans Marge pushed on him.

"She bullied, swore, stamped her feet, and threw a fit like the pirate she was, but Edward didn't back down. He did invite her on a picnic, though."

Jason and I pretended to gag. "Marge doesn't go all mushy, does she?" I asked.

Mrs. Schuster laughed. "Between you and me, maybe a little, but don't tell Marge. She'd never been on a picnic, so she agreed, and before long they were married."

"I knew it! Mush-city." I shivered. "Why do all stories end in marriage? They should have had a duel or something more interesting. But marriage? Eww! She didn't give him the treasure, did she?"

"Why?" Jason asked. "Won't you share your stuff with your husband when you get married?"

I took a swallow of hot chocolate, then wiped my mouth with the back of my hand. "I'm not getting married."

Jason frowned. He turned to Mrs. Schuster. "So what did Marge do? Did she give him the treasure?"

Mrs. Schuster wheezed a laugh. "You two are priceless. No. Marge worried what Edward would think if he found out she'd been a pirate. So she buried it and made a map."

"And she never told him? Her own husband?" I couldn't believe it. Was it even possible to keep a secret that long?

We sat in silence, sipping from our mugs until Mrs. Schuster blew her nose with a great, honking roar. I nearly fell out of my chair.

She dabbed at her eyes and cleared her throat. "You know, my grandmum told me that the secret was Marge's greatest regret. She always meant to tell Edward. It weighed on her. But the time never seemed right."

"Well that's just stupid," Jason said.

I thumped the table. "Yeah. It's not like she stayed a pirate."

Mrs. Schuster stared at us. She opened her mouth, then closed it. Finally she nodded. "You really think that?"

"Well, duh. It's only, like, obvious. And if he left her because of that, then he didn't deserve her anyway."

Jason gasped. "Annie! Look at the clock. We've gotta go. Soccer starts in twenty minutes."

I snatched up the map and we headed toward the door. "I knew Black Marge was real. We wondered at first. But you wouldn't lie to us. You're way too nice."

Jason's cheeks flamed red, as did Mrs. Schuster's. She stared at the floor. "You'd say that about an old woman who chased you out of her yard and took your ball?"

"Well you gave it back. And it's not like you hadn't already warned us."

Mrs. Schuster seemed to consider this. She cleared her throat. "What time do you two leave for school in the morning? You could come for breakfast and I could get you something a little more nutritious than Fruity Discs. And maybe . . . just maybe . . . I could scrounge up a clue or two about that map. Just remember, treasures aren't so easy to find. Even with a map. Believe me, I know."

I hesitated. Visiting from time to time was one thing. But every morning? Still, if we got more clues about the treasure that way . . . well, anything was worth it if Jason didn't have to move. Even if he was stubborn.

I glanced at Jason, who grinned wide. He was nodding.

"It sounds great!" he said.

"But we'd have to ask our moms," I added. What had gotten into him? Was he really that zealous about solving this mystery?

"I'll talk to them. In the meantime, I do have a suggestion for where to look."

"Really? Where?" I gripped the front doorknob, my knuckles turning white. Jason tapped his foot.

"When these houses were built, contractors did an awful lot of digging. Laying pipe, preparing foundations. Seems to me, they dug deep enough to find a treasure if it were in any of those lots."

I gasped. "The empty lot!"

8

We lost our soccer game. Like usual. But with a losing streak as long as ours, it felt comfortable. Like a PB&J for lunch.

And since Jason's dad didn't come (for the third game of the season), my dad treated us to Slurpees. The best part of game day.

When Dad pulled into our driveway, Jason and I ran inside for our weekly contest. We took our positions at the kitchen bar.

"Go!" I said.

We sucked as fast as we could. Fifty points for finishing first. Twenty points for finishing second. Minus ten every time you got brain freeze.

We kept a running total for the season, and so far I was in the lead sixty to forty.

I wasn't even halfway done when Jason squinted in pain. "Owwww!" He pressed his fingers to his head. Amateur.

"Minus ten." I peeked into his cup. He was farther than me, but that didn't matter. I was so going to win.

When he finally opened his eyes, I smiled around my straw. He went at it again, but I could tell he wasn't fully recovered. He wrapped his hands around his head again in less than a minute.

"Minus twenty." I said.

He squinched open an eye to glare at me, but I was already slurping up the dregs.

"I win." I marked my score on our sheet. "You going to finish?"

"Geez. How do you not get brain freeze?" He took a sip of purple slush.

For half a second, I debated telling him my secret, but I decided to hold out. If he moved — which he totally wouldn't — then I would tell him as a parting gift.

While Jason finished his Slurpee, I ran to my room for the map and notebook. I checked the area for spies, but all was clear. Kate and Matt weren't home. I poked my head out the front door, and I could hear my mom and dad chatting as they worked in the garden. Perfect.

I slid back onto my bar stool. Notebook open, I clicked the pen. "So what do we add?"

Jason grinned. "The pills. Seven! Can you believe she takes seven at a time?"

"I know! I can barely scrape down one."

"Add a note to number four and five. Her husband died in ninety-five, and her son played high school football in ninety-five. So he's got to be what?" Jason did the math in his head. "Thirty-six, maybe thirty-seven or thirty-eight."

"Geez. As old as our parents. We can also add that Mrs. Schuster likes her yolks runny. Disgusting!"

Jason frowned. "I doubt it matters how she likes her eggs, Annie."

I looked down my nose at him. As if he's the only one who could add things to our list. "We don't *know* what matters yet. That's why we write down everything. It says so in the Junior Spy Guidebook." I wrote it down in caps.

"Whatever."

We stared at the list, hoping something would jump out at us.

"The pills probably have to do with the heart attack." Jason tapped number six. "You don't think she's dying, do you?"

"Maybe. She is kind of old. But that still doesn't explain why she chose us. Hey! Maybe she *is* dying and since she's mad at her son, she wants to find a new heir for her fortune. She's such a spunky old lady, I bet she wants a spunky heir. That'd be me."

Jason blinked. "Right. Mystery solved. *Not*."

"It *could* be true! All the clues point to it."

"Except the runny yolks."

I stuck out my Slurpee-red tongue. Clearly it was time to change the subject. Flipping the notebook shut, I spread out the map. "So. I had an idea."

"Another one?"

I punched his shoulder. "Mrs. Schuster was right. We haven't checked this thing for hidden clues."

"It's a fake. There are no hidden clues."

I ignored him.

"Do you remember reading about invisible ink? All we have to do is light a candle and hold the map above it. The secret message will just appear. It's brilliant! Just the kind of thing a pirate captain would do."

"You seriously want to mess with fire? After last time?" Jason eyed the scorch mark on the counter where the marshmallow fireball had landed.

"As I recall, you enjoyed those s'mores as much as me. Besides, it's not like anything burned down."

"Lucky for you."

"Anyway, now we're experienced. Practically professionals. And if we hurry, my parents will never know the difference."

"I don't know. Maybe we should get Mrs. Schuster to help us."

"But we're going to the empty lot *today*. We need that message now."

"If there is one," Mr. Gloom-and-Doom said.

I climbed on the counter and pulled down the emergency candle and matches. It had already been used several times, so no one would know we'd lit it.

"Can we at least do it by the sink?" Jason asked.

I rolled my eyes, but I moved the stuff. I guess it was a pretty good idea.

Striking the match against the box, I breathed in the smell of birthdays. Best smell ever. I lit the candle and carefully held the map well above the flame.

A minute passed and nothing happened.

Jason felt the paper. "You're holding it too high. The paper's not even warm."

I lowered it an inch, and Jason snorted. "It has to be near the flames, or it won't work. Plus you have to move it around since a hidden message could be anywhere."

Sweating from the pressure, I held the map closer to the flame. Ever so carefully, I moved it in small circles around every part of the map.

Another two minutes, and still, nothing.

Jason shrugged. "I —"

"Don't you dare say 'I told you so.'" I poked a finger at him.

He rolled his eyes. "I'll save it for when you finally realize there's no treasure."

"Good, 'cause that won't happen." I stuck my tongue out at him.

Jason gasped. "Annie! The map!"

I jerked the thing upward, but it was too late. A hole of fire burst through the center and quickly spread toward the edges. I threw it into the sink, the heat already biting at my hand.

"What do we do?!"

Jason leapt to the faucet and turned it on. Water doused the flames, but the map was ruined. The X was burned out, and the rest was a gushy mess.

Worse, the kitchen now smelled like a full-on campfire. No way my parents would miss this.

"It was nice knowing you."

Now we'd never find the treasure. And I'd be grounded for a month. At least, that's what my parents had threatened after last time.

Jason glanced at the front door. "Quick! Let's clean it up and go to the empty lot now. Maybe the smell will clear out before they come in. Or even better, open a window, and maybe they'll think one of the neighbors lit a fire. Hurry!"

I opened the one above the sink, then picked up the remains of the map. It shredded in my hands.

"No use keeping it now." Jason held out an empty grocery bag.

My stomach sunk to my knees. I wanted to find a way to fix this, but Jason was right. This wasn't fixable. I dumped it in.

Concentrating on the mess, I grabbed a wad of paper towels and wiped out the sink. For good measure, I sprayed it with Windex and wiped it again. Maybe that would mask the burn smell.

Jason dried off the candle and put it back in the cupboard with the matches. I ran to get our bag of supplies while he tied up the evidence. We were halfway down the stairs when I remembered.

"Our lunch! We can't go exploring without a lunch. You go outside and distract my parents. I'll be out in a sec."

I made the fastest PB&Js I've ever made (Jason wouldn't count it because he hadn't been there to time me, but according to the clock, I beat my previous record of one minute and twenty-seven seconds — recorded during our official PB&J Summer Olympics last year — by eight whole seconds!), then placed them carefully in my pack along with two granola bars and two bottles of water. By the time I got outside, Jason had disposed of the goods and convinced my mom to let us borrow her spare gardening spade. It was rusty like nothing, but it would sure dig faster than the plastic yellow shovel in my pack.

Not that we'd know where to dig without the map.

Jason cleared his throat. "Don't you have something to say to your parents?"

I trudged to the garden's edge. "We're going for a walk," I called. "Be back soon." My parents waved and continued working in their precious garden. I shouldn't have worried.

We marched toward the empty lot in silence. I groaned at the thought of the map. How could I have been so careless? And how were we ever going to find the treasure now?

Maybe tonight would be a good time to start Plan C.

9

We rounded the corner past Jason's house, bringing the empty lot in sight. Though the corner of it touched my backyard, we had to walk around the block to get to it. Unless we wanted to crawl under the fence through the ditch. Which sometimes we did, but I didn't need any more ways to get myself in trouble.

We waved to Mr. Garcia, my backdoor neighbor, who returned our greeting from his garage. Not from the regular one attached to his house. From the new monster of a thing he'd built last spring. It even had a car lift.

The story goes that Mr. Garcia inherited a bunch of money from some rich uncle, but my mom insisted he simply saved his money. I liked the first story best.

"Don't look this way while I'm welding!" he shouted. A quick check of his goggles and a flame shot from the welder, sending sparks flying around the hood of the Porsche he was restoring. The one that used to sit on his front lawn.

I kind of envied the guy. He could play with fire whenever he wanted, no threat of being grounded for a month. Then again, he probably wouldn't have turned a treasure map to ash, either. Sigh.

When we got there, we surveyed the lot from the sidewalk. We'd spent a lot of time here, but I'd never thought a treasure could be buried in it. Probably because of all the garbage. It was the only empty lot left in the neighborhood and some builder had used it as a dumping ground. The place was littered with boulders, tree stumps, and old lumber. A few dirt mounds lined one side, and weeds had overgrown the rest, except where some kids had cleared a bike trail.

I kicked at a dirt clod. "Think we can find it without the map?"

"There's nothing to find. The treasure's not real."

"It is!" I punched his arm. "Mrs. Schuster told us it was real to our faces. Besides, what about Black Marge? What more proof do you want?"

"The actual treasure would work." Jason grinned, clearly pleased with his joke. "And I've been thinking about it. Her story doesn't even make sense. If Black Marge was the captain, she had to be old. And suddenly she wanted kids? Right. And how could she have moved that trunk by herself?"

"Mrs. Schuster never told us her age, so you're just guessing. And of course you doubt she could lift it. You're a boy. But who always wins when we arm wrestle, hmm?"

Jason sighed. "Fine. You win. Let's just look for the treasure so we can tell her what we did and get more clues to solve the mystery. Because if I'm right and this story's a sham . . . why would she do that? Why would she lie to two kids and lead them on a wild goose chase? The whole thing gets more mysterious every time we talk to her."

I crossed my arms. "Why would she do that? She wouldn't. And you'll be thanking me when we find the treasure and you get to stay. Just remember that."

"Or," Jason said, *"you'll* be embarrassed when we discover it was all a fake."

I bit back my reply. It's not like we even had a map anymore. I'd made such a mess of things, I wanted to kick myself. No question, this afternoon was going to be a bust. Both in the treasure and fun departments.

I set down my backpack, careful not to smush our sandwiches, and pulled out my mom's gardening spade along with the plastic shovel. I handed it to Jason. I shoved my pack behind some weeds and stood.

"So what do we do?" I asked.

"Just look for an X, I guess." Jason fwipped the plastic shovel against his palm. "We should probably split up so it'll go faster."

"Are you crazy?" We may have been short a map, but that didn't mean we had to throw common sense out the window (my mom's favorite expression). "Don't you ever watch movies? That's the worst thing we can do. Unless we want to die a painful death, we search together."

Jason rolled his eyes. A month ago he wouldn't have. I tried not to think about it.

Side by side, we walked along the cleared-off bike path, searching for that X.

We made it to the mounds on the far side. Still nothing.

"Do you think the smoke smell is gone? How long should we wait before heading back?" Jason glanced in the direction of my house. I was losing him.

"It hasn't been nearly long enough," I said. "Why don't we walk back toward the ditch along the mounds. That'll give us a better view."

"Sure." There was that shrug again.

We slid down the side of one mound, then trooped back up the second. Dirt kept sliding down the side, making the climb harder than it looked. I felt like a real explorer. At the top of the third mound I saw it. "Look!" Two rotting logs lay between the third and fourth mounds, forming a perfect X.

Jason's bored look was gone.

"Those logs look like they've been there a thousand years," I said. "This *has* to be it."

Together we dragged the logs off the spot and dug with all our might. Less than a foot into the hole, Jason's shovel snapped in two. He chucked the pieces into the weeds. "At this rate, we'll never find it."

I wiped at the sweat dripping down my face. "Maybe we could borrow one of your dad's big shovels. It'd go ten times faster."

Jason snorted. "No way I'm asking him. Especially after last night. All he does is yell anymore. He'd just make me clean the turkey pen or something and our treasure hunt would be over. Trust me, it's a bad idea."

"Well we can't go back to my house. We'll just have to take turns with this one." I kept digging. "If we find it, it'll all be worth it."

"Maybe I can find a stick." Jason scrambled up the dirt mound and disappeared down the other side.

I concentrated on shoveling. Each scoop got harder and harder. The spade clinked against rocks and wedging them out was no easy feat. I wiped at the sweat now dripping down my forehead in gallons. This was hard work. And Jason was taking his sweet time looking for a stick. He finally leapt on top of the mound with a small tree branch.

Red berries clung to it like jewels, and Jason thrust it in the air like a scepter. "I'm King of the Hill! All must worship me." He turned in a circle as though greeting his loyal subjects.

I couldn't resist. This was my game. We'd played it a million times before, and I was *good*. I stuck the spade in the dirt and darted up the hill. I meant to bump him softly. Just enough to claim Queendom. But I should have remembered the loose dirt. My feet slipped down the side, and I belly flopped on Jason's legs.

The rest seemed to happen in slow motion. Jason flew backward, arms flailing. He hit the dirt with a thud and his legs flipped over his head into a pile of abandoned lumber. The scream that followed stained my heart.

"My leg!" Jason lay in a heap at the bottom of the mound, half of him buried in wood.

I scurried to his side. "Oh my gosh, oh my gosh, oh my gosh! Are you okay? It was an accident. I swear!"

Jason never cries, but tears streamed down his face. "Get me out, get me out. There's something sharp."

I carefully lifted the top piece of lumber. My stomach flip-flopped when I saw the blood-covered rusty nail. I bit my lip and kept going. Piece by piece, I moved the wood till he was free.

Blood poured down his shin.

With gasping breaths, Jason wiped at the stream with his hands. Red smeared everywhere. He gripped his calf until his knuckles turned white. "Take my sock off." His voice trembled. "Hurry before it gets bloody."

"Who cares about a stupid sock? We need something to stop the blood."

Jason sucked in his breath. "My mom will kill me if I bring home more bloody clothes."

I remembered the acrobat incident two weeks ago. It had been my blood that time, but Jason had heroically offered his shirt to clean up the mess. I pulled off his shoe and sock, then my own. "Hold this while I get the water." I pressed my sock to his shin and ran for my backpack.

I grabbed it and was about to run back when I noticed a tall, pointy-edged plant. The leaves were fuzzy, soft-looking. A memory flashed through my mind of Matt studying for a merit badge: *Aloe is a healing plant with green spiky leaves*. This plant sure fit the description. I grabbed a handful and rushed back to Jason.

Setting the plants aside, I peeled the bloody sock from Jason's leg and poured water over the wound. "The cut isn't that big." I looked hopefully at Jason, who gave me a weak smile. "And I brought a special healing plant Matt told me about." I held it up.

"Maybe you should just get my mom."

I was desperate. The treasure was practically ours. Just a few more feet of digging. And if we went home wounded, we'd never get back. "We don't need your mom. I bet once we rub your cut with this, you'll hardly remember you got hurt. Please?"

"Annie, it's a nail cut. I need to go home."

"Can't we at least try? I promise to get your mom if you still want to after that."

Jason sighed. "Why do I think I'll regret this? Oh yeah, because I usually do."

My fingers tingled. "We have to hurry. My hand is already soaking up the plant's power. I can feel it." I lifted the sock again and rubbed the plant into his shin over his wound. My hand burned, but I wasn't about to say anything. Jason would freak out. I switched hands and bit back the pain. I wiped his shin until Jason jerked away.

"Is it supposed to burn like that?"

Both my hands were burning and itching like crazy, too.

"Of course it is! How else would it heal you?" I pressed the leaves to Jason's shin again.

"This really hurts." Jason's bottom lip trembled.

I lifted the plant, and we gasped.

"What did you *do* to me?" Jason's leg had turned bright red. The skin around his cut was swelling. "Ow, ow, ow! It hurts." Fresh tears streamed down his face. "I want to go home."

The half-dug hole taunted me, daring me to keep going. "But the treasure . . ."

"It's not real, Annie! Grow up!"

I felt like I'd been slapped. Jason never yelled like that.

My hands were on fire, but they didn't hurt half as bad as his words. Tears sprung to my eyes and I stared at the bright red rash blooming on my fingers, trying to pretend that's why I was crying.

Lips trembling, I nodded. "I'll get your mom."

10

"What were you thinking, Annie?" We stood at the bathroom sink while my mom scrubbed my hands with soap.

I ground my teeth against the pain, but it was nothing compared to before.

"You shouldn't have even *been* in that empty lot, but rubbing stinging nettle into that poor boy's leg? Didn't you feel it burning your hands?" She stuck my hands under the tap, then toweled them off with another clean cloth. We had repeated this process every fifteen minutes for the past three hours. I got the lecture at each scrubbing.

"I told you. I thought it was aloe. Matt said it was a healing plant with pointy edges. I thought I was helping." I slumped back onto the closed toilet seat and stared at the pile of used hand towels. It was getting big.

The scene at Jason's house replayed in my mind. His mom had practically gone into hysterics. I could still hear his parents arguing.

"For crying out loud, Bianca, it's just a scratch. He's had his shots. He doesn't need to go to a doctor. You know we don't have money for that!" Mr. Parker had thumped his fist on the table.

"It was a *rusty nail*, Ted. Do you want him to get tetanus? For heaven sakes, just look at it. I'll sell a piece of my jewelry. He's going to the doctor."

When they weren't looking I slipped out and ran home. I was only trying to help. Trying to get them more money. But now I'd made things worse.

The phone rang.

"Don't touch anything." Mom ran to the kitchen. "Hello? . . . Bianca! How is he?"

I sat up and listened hard.

"Wonderful. I'm glad to hear. . . . Uh-huh. . . . I see. . . . No, no. Really, I understand. . . . I can respect that. No need to apologize. . . . And I'll send a note, too. . . . I'm sorry, again. It really was an accident. . . . Are you certain we can't help pay for it? . . . Yes. Okay. Talk to you soon."

I held my breath. But when my mom came back in, my stomach dropped. I knew that look — pity. Not good since she should be mad at me. "What happened?"

Mom took a deep breath. "Jason's going to be fine. He got a shot, and they managed to clean the worst of the stinging nettle out of the wound."

"Can I talk to him?"

My mom shook her head. "Jason's dad is . . ." she cleared her throat, "shall we say upset? You two are grounded from each other for two weeks. And that includes at school."

"What!? But that's not fair." I stared at my mom, hoping it wasn't true.

She slouched against the counter, hand on her cheek. "I'm sorry, Annie. Personally I feel it's a bit harsh, but Mr. Parker . . . well, he has a lot to worry about right now. We have to respect his wishes."

In my mind, Jason yelled at me to grow up. I tried to force back the tears that stung my eyes. They fell anyway. "But we only have a few weeks left. And I didn't even get to tell him I'm sorry." I cursed my chin for trembling. "I didn't get to tell him."

My mom scrubbed more soap into my hands. "I know, honey. I know."

***

I sat cross-legged in the cemetery staring at the uneaten sandwiches from our ill-fated adventure. I'd slipped out as soon as Mom finished with my hands.

The jelly had only seeped through a corner of one sandwich, but it had taken over the other. The print of the water bottle was still visible on that one. Just one more tragedy to add to my tally. But between Jason's leg, my hands, and Mr. Parker's scariness, I'd totally lost my head.

He'd picked Jason up and marched toward home without looking at me.

"Get your stuff," he'd barked.

So I'd grabbed my pack without even thinking about the sandwiches. Plus, I'd had to run to catch up.

And now a burial was required.

I'd never performed the ceremony alone. I wasn't even sure it was possible. The PB&J Society had no rule against it — there'd never been a reason to — but somehow it seemed wrong. Like a PB&J made with apricot jelly.

"I hereby call this meeting of the PB&J Society to order," I finally whispered. "Let the ceremony begin."

This was the part where Jason would inspect the sandwiches. My nose tingled, but I shook it off. I had a duty to perform. Using my wrists, I scooped up the first sandwich and checked it out. "I hereby pronounce this sandwich mold-free and worthy of burial."

I repeated the process for the second one, then grabbed the gardening spade and tried to dig a hole. Using my wrists, I dug at the ground, wincing every time I bumped my hands. I dug and dug until my hands screamed in pain and I had blisters on my wrists.

I stared at my work. The hole wasn't even big enough for a quarter sandwich. I screamed, threw down the spade, and jumped to my feet. I kicked the spade across the cemetery, then raised my foot to stomp the sandwiches to smithereens.

But I couldn't do it.

I dropped to my knees and buried my face in my arms to hide my tears. What had I done? Despite my best efforts to help, I, Annie Jenkins, had made Jason's situation worse. And stomping those sandwiches wouldn't help anything.

I didn't know if Jason would even want to talk to me when our punishment ended, but as a PB&J Society member, I'd have those sandwiches ready for that moment. Because even if there wasn't a rule about not performing the ceremony alone, there should be one. It would be our first order of business.

Not that it would matter if he moved.

A wave of loneliness washed over me. The thought of no Jason left a gaping hole in my life.

I'd promised myself to give up on the treasure. But that didn't mean I had to quit. I thought of my list.

Maybe Plans A and B had failed, but I hadn't even tapped into C and D yet.

I wiped my nose. Put the spade back in my bag along with the sandwiches. The burial would wait. Saving Jason's house wouldn't.

When I got back to my room, I pulled out The List. Holding a pen sent stabs of pain through my bandaged hand, but I no longer cared. I crossed off the failures.

2. Sell appendix on eBay.

Crossed off.

4. Find Jason's dad a job.

Double crossed off.

8. Win a radio contest.

Stupid age discrimination. Crossed off.

But a bake sale could work. Hadn't Mrs. Schuster said my mom's cookies had a reputation? I wrote a big C next to it. And I decided to start Plan D right away, too.

I had to tell my mom about C because I needed her help, but I'd keep Plan D secret. Just in case it didn't work out.

And anyway, it was *my* money.

I pulled out a fresh piece of paper and a pen.

Uncle Jim would help. I was sure of it. Not only did he live in a state with a lottery, but he was the kind of uncle who let you eat ice cream for breakfast. He'd understand . . . and he wouldn't rat me out to my parents.

Though it hurt like crazy to write, I kept at it for twenty straight minutes. Then one last read-through to make sure it was perfect:

Dear Uncle Jim,

You always say that time is money, so I'll get straight to the point. I've got a problem and I think you're the best person to help me. Mostly because you live in Chicago, but also because mom's always saying that you're good with money, if nothing else.

Here's the deal. My best friend in the world has to move. Not because his dad got a new job like you (and we totally miss you, BTW!). Not because he wants to move. But because of money. Which is stupid and unfair if you ask me.

In my generous nature, I have taken it upon myself to earn enough money so they can stay. Unfortunately, since I'm only ten (and FYI, ten-year-olds do NOT like baby dolls as birthday presents), I can't get a job.

I wanted to find one for Jason's dad, but that didn't work out.

I was working on another top-secret project that would have made Jason and me rich enough to take care of it, but that exploded in our faces (well, on my hands and Jason's leg. Kind of hard to explain).

I'd ask for a raise in my allowance, but you know how Mom and Dad are. They'd just lecture me about how money doesn't grow on trees and the value of a dollar, blah, blah, blah. Well, duh. I've known about the tree myth for years, and I'm more than aware of money's value since they refuse to buy me an iPhone.

I'm perfectly willing to sell one of my kidneys (and it's definitely kidney, NOT appendix, in case you were wondering), but come to find out it's illegal since I don't live in Iran. Even on Craigslist. Which strikes me as odd, since it's my body, but there you are.

So you can see, this is my only choice. I'm sending you the $50 I've saved so far for an iPhone. I need you to buy as many lottery tickets as you can.

Let me know how much I won as soon as possible. This is TRIPLE-DECKER urgent!

Love,
Annie.

P.S. Please don't tell Mom and Dad. You know how upset they can get, and I don't want them to worry needlessly. I've always been a caring daughter that way.

P.P.S. Do you think God would help me win more if I'm extra good? . . . I'm pretty good already, but maybe I should throw in a few more prayers. What do you think?

P.P.P.S. Would it be greedy if I kept some of my winnings to buy that iPhone?

I took a deep breath. Straight to the point. Proof I'd already thought through the problem and made my own efforts to solve it. Direct and clear request for help. Precautions against my parents finding out. Check, check, and check. That should do it.

I folded the letter and ran to my parents' room. As usual, Mom was working on bills.

I stuffed the letter behind my back. No need to take chances.

"Mom, I need an envelope and a stamp. And do you have Uncle Jim's address?"

Mom turned around and gave me a funny look. "You wrote a letter to Jim? With your hands like that? Is this a school assignment or something? Why don't you just e-mail him?"

Because I can't send money by e-mail, plus you check my account. I shrugged, going for the innocent look. "I just miss him. And it's always fun to get a letter in the mail. Plus I needed to talk." I gave Mom that look. The one that said I've-just-been-grounded-from-my-best-friend-who-could-be-moving-any-day-and-I-may-not-ever-get-to-see-him-again. Ever.

It worked. For a second. My mom opened a drawer, then paused. "You aren't hitting him up for an iPhone again, are you?"

"Mo-om. It's just a letter." I rolled my eyes, imitating Kate. It always seemed to work for her.

Another suspicious look. Time for a distraction.

"Could I have a bake sale?"

Mom blinked. "What?"

"You know. Sell cookies and stuff. Mrs. Schuster says you're famous, so I bet people would pay lots of money to get one."

"This is about an iPhone." She crossed her arms.

"It's not!" I took a deep breath. Things were going the wrong direction fast. "I want to help pay Jason's doctor bill. Since it was my fault." I hung my head, which I thought was a nice touch.

My mom smiled at me. "That's sweet, honey. But I offered to help pay and they refused."

"So I'll mail the money to them in secret. Please?"

She looked at me then nodded. "How about next Saturday? You'll probably have more luck on a weekend."

"Thank you!" I hugged myself tight while my mom pulled out an envelope and stamps.

So we'd had a setback or two. So what? We were totally going to save Jason's house because these new plans rocked.

Mom held out an envelope. "Here, I addressed it for you. So do I get to read it?"

I blushed, then snatched the offering. "You can't read a letter for someone else. Thanks again about the bake sale!" I bolted before my mom could say anything.

Back in my room, I did a little victory dance.

Wouldn't Jason be surprised when I presented him with a big check so they could keep their house? Or should I give him a briefcase full of cash? Or maybe a swimming pool full, if I got extra lucky.

But I still had work to do. First I needed to finish the letter. Then I could plan next Saturday.

I pulled open my underwear drawer and dug for my savings. I stuffed it all in and pressed the bulging envelope as flat as I could before licking it sealed. Blech. I wiped the horrid taste from my tongue, wishing for the bazillionth time my mom would spring for the self-sticking kind.

As quietly as I could, I snuck out the front door and stuck the letter in the mailbox. The red flag raised, I crossed my fingers.

It hurt to think of the iPhone. I'd have to start saving all over. But if Jason got to stay, the loss was more than worth it.

11

"So you and Jason are grounded from seeing each other." Mrs. Schuster dabbed a linen napkin at her mouth before placing it back in her lap. Unlike our Saturday visit, Mrs. Schuster was dressed and ready for the day.

I pushed pieces of egg around my plate with my fork and nodded. I hadn't intended to visit Mrs. Schuster that morning. Without Jason, the whole thing seemed pointless. But Mrs. Schuster had called our moms with the invitation, like she promised, and our moms determined I should go.

Alone.

Though I'd promised myself not to tell anyone about the stinging nettle, she got the whole story out of me. But I didn't mind. It was nice to have someone listen without scolding for a change.

"I wouldn't have rubbed it on his cut if I'd have known," I said for what felt like the millionth time in the past two days.

"Of course not, dear." She patted my hand.

"And now I can't go back to the empty lot. So if the treasure's there, we might as well give up the hunt. Though . . ." I hesitated. Did I tell her about the map?

It was a priceless artifact, a piece of history, and I had destroyed it. Would she kick me out?

"Yes?" She popped in another bite of egg, clearly unprepared for the magnitude of what I was about to tell her. Maybe that was for the best.

"I, uh . . . I accidently ruined the map."

Mrs. Schuster frowned. "Did it get ripped in all that hullaballoo with Jason? I'm not surprised. Poor boy."

I shook my head. "I lit it on fire," I whispered.

She choked on her bite of egg.

I slouched down in my chair, waiting for the explosion.

"How in tarnation did you manage to burn the thing?" She didn't sound mad, exactly. Though her face was definitely twitching.

"We were searching for hidden messages, like you said. I thought maybe Marge had used invisible ink. But Jason distracted me and it got too close to the flames. And *poof*! The whole thing was gone."

Mrs. Schuster pressed her face into her elbow. Her whole body shook. At first I thought she was shaking with rage (I'd seen that happen when she caught us with the football), but then I realized she was laughing.

It took several moments, but she finally calmed down. "Oh, child. How were we not friends sooner?"

I knew the answer to that one, but I decided not to point out how grouchy she used to be.

"With the map gone, I guess there's no point in searching for the treasure anymore," I said.

Mrs. Schuster sat up straight, suddenly serious. "You know, come to think of it, that map might have been a red herring."

I stared at her, trying to decide if she was serious. "You're saying the map was fish?"

"Red herring. It just means it was a false lead. You know, make people look one place when the treasure is really somewhere else?"

I nodded, though I wasn't sure I understood.

"And actually, I found another clue."

"You did?" I couldn't help myself. Even though I'd sworn off the search, I shivered with excitement. Maybe if I found the treasure, Jason's dad would drop the punishment.

"Yes, and I was wrong about the empty lot. See, I was reading one of Cap'n Black Marge's journal entries."

"She kept a journal? Can I see it?" I imagined a leather-covered pile of parchment roughly sewn together. Just like in the movies. Wouldn't that be just the proof to finally convince Jason the treasure was real? Well . . . as soon as we could speak to each other again.

"Oh, I don't think . . ." Mrs. Schuster looked like I'd asked to play catch with an ancient vase. "It's a bit of a family treasure, you understand. But I can tell you what it said."

"Please? I promise to be careful."

Mrs. Schuster opened and closed her mouth several times. Her teacup full of coffee tinkled against the saucer as she set it down. "I . . . it's . . . um . . . it's really old. Pages crumbling. I keep it in an airtight room and have to wear a special suit. I'm afraid I don't have one your size." She wouldn't look me in the eye.

No one has an airtight room in their house. Well, at least normal people don't. Mrs. Schuster had just lied to me. Jason's words shot through my mind.

Why would she lie to two kids and lead them on some wild goose chase?

I shook the words away. This had nothing to do with the treasure. Mrs. Schuster just didn't trust me with an antique. That's all. Still, that felt kind of cruddy, too.

"But let me tell you what it said." She didn't wait for me to respond. "Not a year after Marge married Edward, her first mate came looking for her. Leonard the Lout."

"Leonard? That doesn't sound like a pirate."

"But he was. The worst kind, too. Would've cheated his own mother for a nickel. But Marge had changed so much by the time he came, she didn't look like a pirate anymore — she wore dresses, no more earrings, actually combed her hair, even spoke differently. They say he bought supplies from her without knowing who she was.

"Still, Marge was worried. Like I said, she hadn't told Edward about her past. So that night, she snuck out, dressed up like her pirate self, and dropped him a visit.

"He demanded the treasure, but Marge refused."

"Why?" I frowned. "I mean, she just buried the thing anyway. It's not like she was using it."

Mrs. Schuster nodded, brow furrowed. She almost looked sad. "True, but she knew Lenny. She knew what he'd do to h– I mean, *with* it. The wealthier a pirate, the more pilfering he can do. The more harm he can cause. Marge had changed, and she couldn't let that happen."

"So what'd she do? Wasn't she scared?"

Mrs. Schuster laughed. "Cap'n Black Marge wasn't captain for nothing. She knew he would come for her when she left. She had a plan.

"See, nothing is more precious to a pirate than his reputation. So before Marge snuck away from her crew, she bought a Brownie camera and took a picture of Leonard the Lout in his sleep.

"She said, 'Unless you ditch this town, and never return, the whole world will know you sleep with a teddy bear and suck your thumb. Hurt me and a hundred copies of your picture will be posted in every known pirate refuge. I've already taken the steps.'"

I snickered. "Really? I like Marge more and more."

Mrs. Schuster beamed. "I thought you would. That's why I gave you the chest."

I caught my breath. *That's* why she gave us the chest? Had I just solved the mystery? But how did she know I'd like Marge? And why was she always inviting us over? Not to mention the pills. I thought of Black Marge's journal, and the lie Mrs. Schuster had just told. She was obviously hiding something. But could the answer be as simple as we reminded her of Marge? That she was lonely?

I sighed. How could I solve any of this without Jason? I hated to admit it, but he might be, *maybe*, better at figuring stuff like this out. Not that I'd ever tell him that. No need to give him a big head.

If there was a chance that treasure was real, I needed to find it. Maybe Plan B hadn't failed just yet.

I pushed my worries aside, determined to see this through. "So what's the clue?"

"She wrote three words on the page in bold lettering: 'ditch,' 'hundred,' and 'steps.' I'd bet she buried that treasure a hundred steps from the ditch."

"But that could be anywhere!" I'd expected something better. Something specific. I slumped in my chair. I couldn't spend all my time counting a hundred steps from every single point of the ditch. And I definitely couldn't dig that many holes. I stared at my still-sore hands.

Mrs. Schuster leaned back, arms folded. "If it weren't for the pictures of pear trees she drew in the margins, I'd agree. But I only know of one house that was built on an old pear orchard."

***

I had been in my new desk a total of two hours and forty-eight minutes and I was ready to scream. Being in the front row stunk like a skunk. And having your best friend as far away from you as possible stunk like a skunk family.

Worse, I was now sitting next to Lila. And she'd had the gall to send me a note.

Dear Annie,

Meet us by hopscotch at recess. Come alone.

The Besties,

L, J&J

The whole thing was written in pink ink and the 'i' was dotted with a heart. And seriously, did they think the teacher wouldn't figure out who wrote the note if they only signed the first letter of their names?

I didn't meet them. And Lila kept trying to catch my eye after that. But I pretended to actually pay attention to Mrs. Starry.

"Annie, you are a model student today. I should have moved you up front sooner!"

I know Mrs. Starry meant that as a compliment, but it was totally embarrassing. If Jason and I could actually talk to each other, he would be mocking me about it the rest of the day. Which was usually my job since he was Mr. Teacher's Pet.

I craned my neck to see if he was watching from his back row seat, but he was bent over his desk, working hard at something. Most likely the writing assignment we were supposed to be doing. I finished mine forever ago, but Jason was a brownnoser. He always wrote until the last second.

The timer on Mrs. Starry's desk clanged. "All right, class. It's lunchtime. Pass your papers to the front of your row. And make sure your names are on them!"

She collected them from my row first.

"Annie, your row may line up for lunch. You'll be first in line today." She smiled her Crest-Strip-white smile and clicked off in her high heels to collect the rest of the papers.

I loved being first, which didn't happen very often because Mrs. Starry liked to dismiss based on behavior. Plus this way, I wouldn't have to stand next to Lila.

I collected my homemade lunch and took my place in the front. That's when I remembered about the extra sandwich. How was I supposed to get it to Jason now?

I glanced back. Jason was last in line. But he wasn't carrying anything. His mom must've forgotten to pack his lunch. So what was he supposed to do? Starve? I needed to get the sandwich to him. And if I happened to slip in an apology for the nail incident, well, that would be a bonus.

We walked toward the lunch room. In my mind I was planning. I could pass the sandwich down the row, student by student. But that's being awfully risky with PB&J — it could very well end up in the cemetery. Or eaten by some rogue kid. I could throw it to him, but that would be assuming he could catch. Not to mention the whole no-throwing-food-in-the-cafeteria rule. They were pretty strict about that. I knew.

In the cafeteria, I took a spot at the table and watched the school-lunch kids file past. I thought maybe I could slip it to Jason when he passed me, but he didn't come straight to the table like usual. Instead, he followed our classmates to the cafeteria line.

I couldn't eat. I watched him pick up a tray and choose the pre-fabbed selections for the day. When he reached the lunch lady, he said something and she punched some keys on the register. She nodded and it was done.

Jason was officially a turncoat. I blamed myself. He probably hated my guts after what happened and was making a statement. I couldn't even resent him for it. I'd be mad, too, if *he* had pushed *me* onto a nail.

When Lila and her posse banged down their trays just across from me, I nearly jumped out of my skin.

"Trying to catch flies?" Jess asked and they all giggled at their *hilarious* joke. Yeah. And they wondered why I didn't bother to meet them at recess.

I closed my mouth and pointedly ignored them. I left Jason's PB&J in the bag and lined up the rest of my food, hoping they'd take the hint.

They didn't.

"So where's your boyfriend?" Lila asked.

My eyes betrayed me. I glanced at the other end of the table, which of course Lila noticed.

"Oh. Did you break up?"

Her feigned concern could have gagged a whale. Where was a dish full of Vegetable Yuck when you needed it? Getting struck with Jason's PB&J would be too great an honor for her.

"He's not my boyfriend, and we didn't have a fight. We're just grounded from each other." Aaack. I hadn't meant to explain anything.

Lila's hand flew to her mouth, while Jess and Jen squealed in unison. They grabbed each other's hands.

"Just like Romeo and Juliet! That is SO romantic." Lila leaned forward. "You have to tell us everything. Come over after school. All of you." The girls all nodded, leaning in to invade my personal space. I nearly fell off the bench trying to breathe.

"And oh yeah! Then I can show you my new Prada purse. Daddy surprised me with it!"

Jess and Jen squealed again.

"Oh my gosh!"

"You are so lucky!"

I wanted to puke. Not even PB&J was worth this. And looking at a purse? I'd rather eat Vegetable Yuck. I piled my stuff back into the sack. "Sorry, I'm grounded." I marched toward the playground doors, relieved to get away.

Before going out, I threw one last glance at Jason. He was finally looking at me. His gaze dropped to my lunch then back to my eyes with an intensity I knew. I blinked and he was hunched over his lunch like none of it had happened.

My heart nearly leapt out of my throat. Maybe he didn't hate me!

I ran for the baseball bleachers, then tore into my lunch. Something was there. Something from Jason. I just knew it.

I wanted to shout when I found the note. It was short, but I didn't care. It was from Jason.

Annie,

Sorry about my dad and that I yelled at you. It's not your fault. I'm fine. Keep getting clues so we can solve the mystery.

Jason

P.S. Keep up the good work, model student! ha ha

P.P.S. This note will self-destruct in 5 seconds (hint, hint).

My chest didn't feel as tight anymore. Even if he had insulted me, it felt good. Almost like we weren't grounded. Almost.

And Jason didn't hate me!

I wanted to keep it, but Jason was right. We couldn't risk getting caught. I shredded the paper into tiny bits and buried them in the dirt below the bleachers. Which is totally not littering since paper used to be dirt anyway. Or something.

Pounding the dirt flat, I took a deep satisfied breath. I could get through this. Because I had a mission to accomplish for my still-best friend.

12

After school I wanted to head straight to the ditch once I'd stowed the uneaten PB&Js with the other two. But Mom made me do my homework. I practically broke the door when I tore out of the house. Only one pear tree remained in the neighborhood — in my backyard! How awesome would it be to find the buried treasure there? Then no one could claim it didn't belong to me.

Starting at the ditch, I lined myself up with the tree. True, this had been a whole orchard of trees back then, but you have to start somewhere. At least this would give me an idea. I counted each step from the water's edge.

One . . . Two . . . Three . . .

. . . Ninety-four . . . Ninety-five . . .

I couldn't go any farther. The stupid fence between my house and Jason's blocked me. I peeked through the slats and imagined five more steps, hoping, hoping, hoping five steps would be enough.

It wasn't. Five steps put me smack in the middle of the turkey pen.

Gobble, gobble!

A turkey pecked at me through the fence and a memory of fast-moving feathers and a beak flashed through my mind. I fell flat on my rump trying to get away.

I shivered at how close the thing had been. Stupid birds that attacked innocent children for no reason. I still resented Mrs. Gibbs, my kindergarten teacher, for taking us on that Thanksgiving field trip. And I resented all those people who made a big deal about the Parkers' organic turkeys.

It took everything I had not to be grateful the things would be gone soon.

But that meant Jason would be gone, too. That couldn't happen. And though I would rather spend time with Lila than face a turkey, I had no choice. I had two weeks to work up the courage. Two long weeks without Jason.

What was I going to do with all that time? There was the bake sale to plan, but that wasn't until Saturday. For as long as I could remember, Jason and I had spent every possible waking moment together.

I had other friends, but they all lived far enough away that getting together took effort. Suzie only lived a mile away, but my mom didn't think I was old enough to ride my bike there on my own. And I couldn't be bothered with planning something in advance. That took all the fun out of it. Unfortunately, parents can be pretty fussy about things like that.

I stared across the yard, looking for something to do. The trampoline. That would be fun. Trying to catch the excitement, I ran to it and vaulted on. I jumped as high as I could, stretching to go just a little higher. Once, Jason had challenged me to a contest to see who could jump highest.

After letting me go first, he'd cheated by tucking up his legs. We still didn't agree on who'd won.

I stopped bouncing. Geez. Now I was missing his annoying habits.

I tried harder to have fun. I did a flip, a cartwheel, every trick I knew. I practiced back drops, belly drops, knee drops, seat drops, and every other drop I could think of.

It was boring without Jason. No contests. No one to make me laugh.

One last back drop and I let myself bounce to a stop. I stared at the clouds and smiled at the first shape I recognized: a PB&J. A small puffy cloud next to it looked like a blob of jelly that had dribbled out. "Look at . . ." I had forgotten. No Jason.

"Get off, cheesebreath. My friends and I want to bounce."

I rolled over to face Matt and two of his geeky friends. "I was here first."

"You're just lying there. You can do that on the grass." Matt hopped onto the tramp and started bouncing me.

I shot to my feet to defend my rights when the idea struck. "I'll let you jump if I can jump, too."

Matt's friends climbed on.

"No way, little sis," Matt said. "We're playing WWE and you'd get squashed, right Jimmy?"

"Like a bug, squirt." Jimmy pounded a fist into his palm.

I scowled at him. He was skinny with greasy hair. Something about him creeped me out. "Trust me, I'm just watching out for you." Matt drove his shoulder into Jimmy's and the two of them landed in a heap.

"Body slam!" Matt's other friend charged at me.

I leaped off the tramp just in time. Arms folded, I watched them plow into each other, debating if it was worth the fight.

It wasn't. Not without Jason.

With the grunts and laughs from Matt and his friends in the background, I wandered toward the ditch. An African jungle safari would at least be peaceful. I sat to pull off my shoes, but never got that far. It just wasn't the same without Jason.

How was I going to get through two more weeks? Let alone if he moved. That would be a disaster. We *had* to save his house. The treasure was still a possibility, plus I had the lottery tickets coming, not to mention the bake sale. But maybe it was time to work on Plan E. Just in case.

"Pipsqueak! We need a third. You want to play?" Kate and her friend Emma stood over me. Despite my crisis, I jumped up. Kate *never* invited me to play. "Really?"

"Really." Kate stopped a few feet away to pull off her shoes.

"But you have to do exactly what we say," Emma said. "No questions."

I couldn't believe my luck. "Okay." Maybe today wouldn't be so bad. And maybe they'd let me hang out tomorrow, too, once I'd proven how cool I was.

"We're playing Castaway," Kate said.

"Like Gilligan's Island?" Dad bought the DVD sets of every season. I knew all about castaways.

"Exactly." Kate's smile got bigger.

"The thing is," Emma said, "a terrible disease is killing off the castaways. So you have to lie down and stay perfectly still."

"So I'm dead?" I didn't like the sound of that, but no way was I going to complain.

"Of course not! What would be the point of that?" Kate snapped. "Remember? No questions."

"Sorry." I hurried to lie down.

Kate sighed. "We're in the middle of a tragedy." She wiped a pretend tear from her eye. "There are so many dead bodies, we don't know who's alive and who's dead. There's only one way to find out." Kate gripped my wrists as Emma grabbed my legs. Lifting me off the ground, they ran for the ditch.

I screamed. "Mom!" I squirmed and kicked as hard as I could, but they were too strong. "I'll tell Mom!"

Kate laughed. "I thought you wanted to play with us. Be involved in our lives. Read our journals."

I froze. Oh no. How could I have let my guard down?

"What? Did you think I forgot, you little spy?"

Water crept up my back. I twisted as hard as I could.

"I'm warning you . . . let me go!" I tried to spit at Kate, but it landed on my cheek.

Kate shrugged. "If you say so." They dropped me in the ditch and scampered away laughing.

I was drenched. And furious. I kicked as much water at them as I could, but they were too fast. "You'll be sorry!" I yelled as they rounded the corner of the house.

Sloshing across the backyard, plans for revenge swirled through my mind. Grasshoppers in Kate's bed? A mouse would be better if I could find one. I nearly laughed at the thought of Kate's face when she pulled down her covers.

Matt's friends guffawed as I passed the tramp. They reminded me of monkeys.

"That's a nice look!" Matt laughed.

"Come closer and say that!" I shook my head, flipping water their direction.

"Oooh! She likes us." Jimmy puckered his lips and opened his arms.

I glared, then stomped off. My hair whipped my cheek, but I ignored it. Mom would sympathize. Then she would punish Kate.

"Annie?" Lila stood by the corner of my house, clutching a purse.

Geez. Of course she'd show up at my house that very moment. Why wouldn't she? No other moment would have been nearly as embarrassing.

I sloshed toward her, daring her to make fun of me. "What?"

"Are . . . are you okay?"

"Do I look okay?" I spread my arms wide, splashing water at her.

She clutched her purse tight and stepped back. "Oh, well . . . I came to show you my Prada purse since you were grounded, but . . ." Her voice trailed off and she didn't even try to show the thing to me.

I raised my eyebrows.

"Maybe I'll try again later when you're . . . better?"

I didn't bother to reply. I simply turned and climbed the porch stairs, shoes squishing with each step.

"Mom?" I stood on the doorstep waiting, but no answer. That's when I saw it. On the counter sat a half-prepared casserole. Broccoli casserole. It was a conspiracy!

I wanted to scream. This was the worst day ever! I decided not to care about the wet footprints. I stomped to my room and slammed the door.

The whole thing was so unfair. Forced off the tramp, bullied into the ditch, my humiliation witnessed by Lila, and now broccoli casserole waiting to comfort me. Well no thank you!

By the time I'd changed, I had an idea. What if I just didn't go to dinner? What if I pretended to be asleep? It could work.

Before anyone found me, I jumped into bed and pulled up the covers. They felt warm and cozy after the cold, wet ditch. I closed my eyes and imagined the moment when Jason and I could dig up Black Marge's treasure.

Jason's dad would smile like he used to and tell Jason how proud he was. My mom would say, "That's our Annie!"

But then Leonard the Lout appeared, and he looked a lot like Matt's greasy friend. "That thar treasure be mine. Arrrgh! Hand it over or ye'll be walkin' the plank."

He pointed at a diving board attached to my back porch. Instead of my yard, a massive broccoli casserole sloshed below with bright green broccoli monsters leaping out of the sauce. They snapped their teeth at me in anticipation.

But I knew what Leonard would do to the treasure. I took a daring step forward to face him, but Jason cut between us. He held out red, swollen hands. "I've got the curse! Come any closer and I'll touch you. You'll be branded with cooties the rest of your life."

Leonard shuffled backward. He turned to run when Mrs. Schuster grabbed him by the ear and dragged him away. "You just leave town before my Ned hears about you."

I stirred from my dream. My parents' voices crept into my mind.

"No, don't wake her. I wonder if she's coming down with something. She was dragging through the house earlier. I thought she was just moping about Jason."

"Well, I guess we can tell the kids after she wakes up."

I snuggled into my covers. *Tell us what?* I wondered, but I was already back at the treasure chest.

★★★

When I woke up, I heard the clanging of dishes. I smiled as I wandered from my room, rubbing my eyes.

"Sleeping Beauty's awake." Dad stuck a plate in the dishwasher.

"Dad! You're home early." I ran to give him a hug.

"I missed you, too, sweet pea."

"How are you feeling?" Mom asked.

"Fine. But I guess I missed dinner." I hung my head.

"You did, but we saved you a plate." Mom opened the microwave, but it was empty. "It was right here. Sam, did you see a plate of food when you were clearing the table?"

Dad adjusted his glasses. "Was that for Annie?"

"Oh, Sam, you didn't."

He reached for mom's hand. "You know I can't resist your broccoli casserole."

I could have kissed him. Home early one time and already he was saving the day. I wished he could be home more often.

Mom snapped the dish towel at him with a grin and then turned to me. "So, what to get you for dinner? Cereal? Peanut butter and jelly?"

"Or," Dad interrupted. "Since this is my fault, maybe I could take you to McDonald's."

My grin must have reached my ears. I couldn't believe my luck. Finally, after such a rotten week, my plans were working out perfectly.

Mom leaned against the counter. "Tonight? We had other plans. Remember?"

"Then let's take all the kids. Ice cream cones for everyone. We can tell them there."

Mom sighed. "Fine. Let me get my purse. We can finish the dishes later."

Ten minutes later, the minivan pulled into the parking lot. Kate glared at Mom and Dad. "This is so unfair!" she said for the fifteenth time. "Why does she get McDonald's when the rest of us had to have broccoli casserole?"

Dad just smiled. "You're right. It's not fair. Poor Annie missed out on your mom's delicious meal and has to settle for McDonald's. I appreciate your concern for your sister, though."

I couldn't have planned a better revenge. The memory of Kate's face would get me through a year of teasing. I only wished I had a camera.

Matt jostled me when he climbed out and threw me a dirty look, but I didn't care. *I* got McDonald's.

Once we were seated in the round booth, I did my best to make the meal last as long as possible. I was nibbling the edges of my last nugget when Dad cleared his throat, a serious expression on his face.

"Your mom and I have something to tell you."

Kate sat up straight, horror written on her face. "Is this about that 'meeting' at the hospital? You're not going to tell us Mom's pregnant, are you?" She slumped in her seat. "This keeps getting better and better."

Matt squirmed. "Good thing I already finished my ice cream or I might be sick."

I grinned. Finally! Someone *I* could boss around.

Mom sighed. "No, I'm not pregnant. I'm going back to work at the hospital. I start training in two days, then I'll be on the night shift starting next week."

I choked on my last bite. "But who's going to take care of us? Make our lunches? Wash our clothes?" The nuggets I'd eaten suddenly felt like rocks in my stomach. In one fell swoop, my perfect revenge was ruined.

Dad laid a hand on my shoulder. "That's the good news. I was laid off from my job today, so I get to stay home with you."

13

I crawled out from behind Mrs. Schuster's rose bush and held up a fistful of weeds. "You were right. There were a lot back there." I chucked them at the already-full bucket.

Mrs. Schuster sat back on her foam pad and wiped at her forehead. "Ned would be horrified at how far I've let this patch go. It was always his favorite. But I don't have the energy to keep up with everything anymore. Just don't tell my son that."

"Well it looks good to me. If you hadn't asked me to go back there, I'd never have noticed. No one would have."

"But I'd have known," Mrs. Schuster said. "So thank you for helping. I couldn't have gotten them myself."

I crouched down to examine the flowerbed Mrs. Schuster was weeding. "My mom always wished her flowers could look like yours. But I guess that won't happen now." I brushed a finger across a purple flower, trying to ignore the lump forming in my throat.

"Want to talk about it?"

I kept my eyes on the dirt, searching for the tiny weeds Mrs. Schuster insisted were killing the flowers. Complaints buzzed through my mind, but I shook my head.

Only day two of mom at work, and already I was sick of it. No fresh-baked cookies waiting when I got home from school. No mom to make math homework fun. I could barely stand to think about the things in my lunch Dad tried to pass off as peanut butter and jelly sandwiches. It was just as well Jason didn't need that second one anymore. And though I'd saved them with the others, I doubted they'd even qualify for the cemetery.

At least I had the bake sale. Mom had promised she didn't have to work.

Still, thank goodness for Mrs. Schuster. Though I'd have died laughing if someone told me a week ago I'd think that.

"You know, you and Cap'n Black Marge have a lot in common."

I frowned. "Why? Did her mom have to work?"

Mrs. Schuster chuckled. "I meant that she faced some rotten situations, too. But she always came out on top."

"You mean like the time those rival pirates threw her and her crew into the brig of her own ship?" Mrs. Schuster had told me the story yesterday, at breakfast. "They really should have made sure they took all the keys from her first."

"In their defense, Marge did hide it pretty well." Mrs. Schuster pulled off her gardening gloves. "And did I tell you? After that, her crew thought she was a genius, plus she doubled their treasure by claiming the bounty on those thugs. So, see? Good from a bad situation."

I shrugged. "I guess, but I just don't see any good from my mom going back to work." Or Jason moving.

"Well, keep your eyes peeled. You never know when that good will happen. For now, I think we're finished here. Shall we go eat those cookies I promised? And perhaps another round of Mancala? I still can't believe you beat me your first time playing."

"Sure." I hopped up and gathered the tools we'd used. It was nice to have something besides my mom to think about. Even though Mancala was a crazy old game — not electronic *at all* — it was still cool. Plus, Mrs. Schuster claimed Black Marge got the set on one of her trips to Africa.

It wasn't very often you got to play with an ancient relic. Jason would be jealous. At least he would be as soon as I was allowed to talk to him again. Only nine days to go. Two hundred and eight hours. Twelve thousand four hundred and eighty minutes. But who was counting?

"Annie!" Dad stood at the end of our yard. "Time for dinner! Plus you have soccer tonight. We need to hurry!"

My stomach flip-flopped. Soccer practice. With Jason. I grinned.

I waved at my dad. "I'll be there in a minute!" When Dad went back inside, I apologized to Mrs. Schuster. "I forgot about soccer. Can we play tomorrow?"

"I'll be here." She bent down and whispered in my ear. "Should I sneak you some rations? Or do you think he'll do better this time?"

121

I laughed. "If you hear a tap on your window later, you'll know why."

When I got home, I was surprised by how good it smelled. Like something Mom would have made. After yesterday's "blackened" barbecue chicken and broccoli mush, I didn't think Dad was capable of making anything that smelled this good.

I ran up the stairs ready to eat, but I was annoyed to find Dad just standing behind Kate at the piano. Kate was playing Moonlight Sonata for about the billionth time.

"I thought you said dinner was ready!"

Dad just waved me off. "I'm listening," he mouthed.

I glared at his back. When Mom called us for dinner, it was on the table. And hadn't he said we were in a hurry?

"Watch out, cheesebreath!" Matt pushed past me and headed for the kitchen. He had an air-filled bike-tire tube in his black, greasy hands.

I followed him and watched as he smeared black all over the handles of the kitchen faucet.

"Mom's gonna be mad," I informed him. "You know she doesn't let you . . ."

"Mom's not here, is she?" Matt didn't look up. He rotated the tire through the water-filled sink. "Ah-hah! There you are." Splashing water onto the floor, he grabbed a dish towel and rubbed it on the tire before marking it with a pen.

I gaped at the black streaks on the white cloth, then folded my arms. "But Dad is. You are *so* dead."

Matt rolled his eyes. "Wanna bet on that, sis?" He shouldered his way past harder than he needed to and bounded down the stairs.

I didn't even notice Kate had stopped playing until Dad spoke. "Did you know he can change a tire in five minutes flat? Pretty awesome. I asked him to fix all those bikes I've been meaning to get to. Now you can ride your bike again. Isn't that great?"

"But Mom never lets him use the kitchen sink. Especially not at dinner! And did you see what he did to her dishcloth?"

Dad ruffled my hair. "You inherited your mom's worrying, didn't you? Dishcloths wash, and I told him to use the kitchen sink because it's the best one for fixing tires. Now let's eat so we can get you to soccer practice."

My stomach swirled. Suddenly I didn't feel hungry. And this time it was *before* seeing what Dad had made.

"Move it or lose it, squirt." Kate flipped her hair in my face and flounced to the kitchen. "Some of us have lives."

"Now, Kate." Dad gave her a look, then turned to the Crock-Pot on the counter. "Your mom started her famous chicken noodle soup before she left this morning, so dinner should be better today. All I had to do was add the noodles, which I did first thing this morning."

"It sure smells better," I said.

Dad dunked a ladle in the pot, then pulled it out frowning. "What the . . . ?" A big mass of something grayish oozed yellow slime back into the Crock-Pot.

"What is that?" Kate asked.

"That doesn't look like Mom's soup," I said.

"But I followed her instructions!" Dad picked up the note. "See? Just add the noodles from the freezer. Right there."

Kate looked at the note. She rolled her eyes. "Geez, Dad. It says 'Just add the noodles from the freezer *one hour before eating.*' Didn't you read the whole thing?"

Dad's shoulders drooped for a second, then he perked back up. "So the noodles are mush. Big deal. The soup part will still taste the same." He plopped the gray mass into the sink, then dunked the ladle again. This time it held thick, yellow pudding with orange and green blobs.

Matt barged into the kitchen and skidded to a stop. "What is that?"

Kate and I shared a look. Which was kind of weird because that just doesn't happen. "That's supposed to be Mom's chicken noodle soup," she said.

"Cereal again? I vote yes." Kate was already pulling out the Sugar-dusted Wheat Squares.

"Well, I'm having soup. You kids are just too picky." Dad plopped the pudding into a bowl and took a big, fat bite. After taking an exceptionally long time to swallow, he dumped the stuff into the sink. "Can you pull out the Wheaties, Kate?"

14

Saturday morning was supposed to be exciting. The first day Mom had off since she started working, *and* the bake sale. But Mom came to breakfast in scrubs.

My spoon clinked against my bowl when I dropped it. "You have to work?"

The toaster popped and my mom pulled out a piece of toast and buttered it. "I'm sorry, Annie. A friend needed the day off and I was the only one available. But it means I'll have an extra day off next week. Won't that be nice?"

"But today's the bake sale! You told me you didn't have to work and I've already posted fliers around the neighborhood. Have you even made any cookies yet?"

"No cookies, sis. Trust me, I would have eaten them if she had." Matt stuffed a bite of Fruity Discs in his mouth.

Mom frowned. "Don't tease, Matt. And Annie, as I recall the bake sale is your project, not mine. You're ten. It's time you started pitching in more."

"How can I make cookies if you don't let me use the oven?" I crossed my arms, and my spoon, along with a bunch of milk, flew out of my bowl.

Kate's chair squealed when she scooted back from the table. "Watch it, squirt! Some of us care how we look."

"Oh, Annie." Mom hurried a paper towel to me. "Clean up your mess, please."

I mopped up the milk, scowling the whole time.

"What's the problem?" Dad entered the kitchen and kissed Mom on the cheek as he stole a piece of her toast. "Thank you, m'love."

Mom sighed. "Today is supposed to be Annie's bake sale. With all the training videos I've had to watch, I just forgot to make cookies."

Dad shrugged. "I can help. What time's the bake sale?"

"One o'clock," I said. But I didn't want Dad's help. I wanted Mom's. The posters advertised "Mrs. Jenkins's" cookies. Not Mr. Jenkins's. I glowered at the paper napkin.

"And maybe Kate can help, too," Dad said.

Kate carried her bowl to the sink. "Sorry. Emma and I are working on a history project at her house. It's worth one-third of our grade."

"Matt?"

"No can do, *mi padre*. I'll be mowing the lawn. Which reminds me. I'd like payment in full before this evening, please. Jimmy and I are going to the movies."

Mom had pulled out a cookbook and was flipping through the pages. "And what movie might that be?"

"Oh you know, some R-rated movie full of blood and guts and violence."

Mom gave him the look.

"Kidding! Just don't forget the money. I was serious about that."

126

Mom sighed, then plopped the book in Dad's arms. "Here. Here's my recipe that gets all the compliments."

He set it on the counter. "Well this doesn't look hard."

I should have canceled the bake sale right then. But Jason's house was on the line. Plus, Mom got us started on the recipe. She even explained the thing, word by word. Surely Dad couldn't mess that up, could he?

We mixed dough right up until it was time to leave for my game. The first time I've wished the game would just hurry and end. But Jason wasn't there, and I had to deal with Lila, who suddenly thought she was my new best friend what with Jason out of the picture. She was on me before the game even began.

"So I saw your flier and had the most fabulous idea! I could totally join you. My mom has the best recipe for lemonade. And then you wouldn't have to sit there alone. Plus you'd make a ton more sales in front of my house than yours." She flipped her blond, ponytailed ringlets back as if they had anywhere to go.

I watched them bob up and down before finally responding. "What about Jessica and Jenny? Don't you have plans?"

Lila dismissed the idea with a wave of her hand. "Oh, they have some big dance competition in the city today. I was going to go with them, but they said no non-dancers allowed. You know how it is."

Right. So she wanted in 'cause she was bored? Um, yeah. Let me think. "No thanks. I've got it covered."

Which I totally didn't, but no sense giving Lila a front row seat to watch my plans implode. Lucky for me the coach gathered us in for our pre-game pep talk just then.

Coach thumped his clipboard like he always did to fire us up. "Okay guys. I want you to go out there and play your best!"

I snuck a peek at Lila, who frowned when she noticed me. Her eyes narrowed, and I suddenly had a feeling something bad was about to happen. But I wasn't worried, because what could possibly be worse than "the haircut"?

After forty minutes of nine-to-zero humiliation, my dad and I rushed home to finish getting ready for the bake sale. Dad baked the cookies, while I made the price list. Luckily I was good at math, so I easily calculated the price per cookie to make this whole thing worthwhile.

Looking back, I should have brought the paper and markers into the kitchen, but I didn't think about it until the burnt smell hit my nose.

"Please let Matt be making toast!" I prayed. Poster in hand, I rushed to the kitchen where my worst fears stared back at me like beady little bug eyes. Dad held two pans of black hockey pucks instead of the cookies I expected.

"What did you do?!"

Dad slid the pans onto the stove and closed the oven. "Okay. Just stay calm. This isn't as bad as it looks."

"Not as bad as it looks?" How could he even say that?

"Well, I mean . . . we could maybe dip them in chocolate or peanut butter, and . . . and . . ."

"And call them chocolate-covered ashes? Dad! How could you do this? Mom gave you exact instructions!"

Dad wiped the sweat off his forehead. "I know she did, but I calculated it out, and we didn't have time to do ten batches at twelve minutes each. So I increased the temperature, decreased the time, and thought I'd outsmart the system by doing four pans at once."

That's when I noticed the other two pans on the counter. Those cookies weren't completely black like the others, but definitely not edible.

"Oh, and I might have gotten a little sidetracked making you a cool stand to sell the cookies from. It's in the garage. You should see it!"

"What good is a stand with no cookies?" My nose prickled, and that spot behind my eyes burned.

"I'm sorry! I thought I could handle both. But on the bright side, we still have more cookie dough." He pushed his glasses up his nose and looked at me all hopeful-like.

Mouth clamped shut, I nodded. I didn't trust myself to speak. But what had I expected? That my dad would suddenly be able to cook?

Dad cleared his throat and pointed to my poster. "So uh, you might want to lower that price a bit. I just don't see anyone paying twenty dollars for one of these."

But they would've for Mom's. This whole mess was her fault! How could she abandon me like this?

I looked at the clock. We only had twenty minutes left. Not quite two batches. The whole thing seemed pointless now. But then I thought of Mrs. Schuster and Black Marge. The pirate captain always found good in a bad situation. Was that possible?

Dad slid the hockey pucks from the pan to the cooling rack, and suddenly an idea struck.

First I marched to the oven and adjusted the temperature. "This time, we follow Mom's instructions. One batch at a time."

"Agreed."

"And don't throw those cookies away. I have an idea."

I hated to do it, but I needed Matt's help. After searching the house with no luck, I called Jimmy's.

"What do you want, pipsqueak?" Matt sounded annoyed.

As fast as I could, I explained the street hockey idea to him. "Please? I'll share the profits."

The line was silent for a moment. "Not just profits," he finally said. "Make it a base price of ten dollars even if no one plays, plus fifty percent. Then I'm in."

I bit my lip. That sounded like a lot. But half a cookie would cover the ten dollars. And it's not like I had many options. "Fine. But only fifty percent of the game profits. Not on the cookies."

"Deal. See you in five."

I hoped I hadn't just made a big mistake, but I didn't have time to worry about it. First I fixed the poster:

Mrs. Jenkins's Famous Cookies + Cookie Street Hockey
$20/cookie OR $2/game

Dad used a furniture dolly to move the cookie stand to the corner of our cul-de-sac and staple-gunned the sign to it. With no time to spare, we Saran-wrapped the fresh-baked cookies. To give Dad credit they weren't burned this time. They just looked more like miniature cow pies than chocolate chip cookies. As long as they didn't taste like cow pies, I no longer cared.

By the time we got outside, Matt had set up his practice goal and was shooting pretend pucks into it.

I even smiled when Dad set the plate of blackened cookies on the table. Talk about making lemonade out of lemons. If Jason and I weren't grounded from each other, we'd be laughing like crazy about the whole thing.

That was when the Pierces' garage door opened. Suddenly I didn't like my little lemon analogy anymore. Lila wheeled out a professional-looking, white-painted lemonade stand and waved all friendly-like at my dad.

"Hi, Mr. Jenkins!"

I was about to tell her off when my dad answered her, the traitor. "Well hello, Lila! What a nice addition to Annie's bake sale. Do you need any help?"

My mouth dropped open. Didn't he see this for the hostile takeover it was?

"Thank you, but I can do it on my own."

Dad nodded, then turned to me. "I'll keep baking more of those cookies, sweet pea. Good luck!"

Lila made a few more trips inside, and her stand was complete. A glass pitcher of lemonade with lemon wedges floating alongside the ice. A bowl of lemons and a cute little sugar bowl, with a cute little spoon. A pile of crystal-clear plastic cups, and under it all a frilly tablecloth that matched the lacy pink dress Lila wore.

As if clothes mattered. I was still in my sweaty soccer uniform. Because I was selling cookies. Not clothes. Sheesh.

But I felt better when she taped up her price: $1.00 per glass. Pssht. No way she'd make any money with a price like that.

When Lila finally sat down, I stuck my tongue out at her. She threw one of her snobby looks at me and pretended to act all sweet. What a fake!

When the first customer arrived at my stand (not hers), I smiled wide. It was Mrs. Schuster.

"Like the reformed crabby woman I am, I came to show my support." She was all dressed up and even wore a hat with a huge blue feather on it that matched her purse. The funniest part was that she carried a cane. She just didn't use the thing.

I beamed at my friend. "Thanks, Mrs. Schuster! What can I get you?"

She looked down at my offerings and started coughing. "And you say these are your mother's cookies?"

I cleared my throat. "Well, it's her recipe anyway. She kind of had to work at the last minute."

"Hmm. Well a word to the wise. Maybe you should wrap them in some tinfoil, too." She opened her purse and pulled out her wallet. "So how much will one of these cookies set me back?"

I pointed to the sign, and Mrs. Schuster started coughing again. "My, my, my. Inflation's a killer, isn't it? Any chance you'd give an old lady a senior's discount? I only have a five dollar bill." She pulled it from her purse and held it out.

Losing fifteen dollars on the first sale didn't bode well, but no way was I going to let Lila think no one wanted my goods. I took the money and handed Mrs. Schuster a cookie.

"There you go. Thank you SO MUCH for your business." I might have spoken a little louder than I needed to.

Mrs. Schuster unwrapped the cookie and took a bite.

"Oh." She stopped chewing and held a hand to her mouth. "Oh my." She looked around and caught sight of Lila's stand. "Excuse me." She stuffed the cookie in her purse and started pulling quarters from her wallet as she rushed across the street.

I watched her gulp the whole thing down in seconds. And as if that wasn't bad enough, she bought a second one!

When she finally headed home, she waved. "Good luck with the bake sale."

I glared at Lila, who waved with that sticky-sweet smile on her face. She was such a phony! How did people not see it?

But they didn't. Even though I stayed at my stand for over two hours, not one more person bought a cookie. I even tried the tinfoil trick Mrs. Schuster had suggested. No luck. Because they were all too busy buying lemonade across the street. A few boys wandered over to play Cookie Street Hockey, but that was it.

When it was all over, Matt helped me carry everything back inside. I thought he was just being nice until he demanded his money.

"Time to pay up, pipsqueak. Five hockey customers at two dollars a pop makes ten, so at fifty percent you owe me five dollars of that, plus a ten-dollar base fee for a grand total of fifteen dollars. I should charge you a set-up and take-down fee, but I'm feeling generous today." He held out his hand.

"Fifteen dollars? But that's all I even made!" I pulled the crumpled bills from my pocket and lay them on the kitchen counter.

His face got all serious as he straightened them out and counted. "Yup, that's fifteen all right." He stuffed the money in his back pocket and headed to his room laughing. "Nice doing business with you, sucker!"

I climbed onto a stool and lay my head on the counter. What a rotten day. All that work, and nothing to show for it. Except a bunch of burnt cookies and a sloppily-made sign. And one more item to cross off the list. What a waste of a Saturday.

My dad cleared his throat from behind.

"What?" I moaned.

"We were in such a hurry this morning, we never did get our traditional game-day Slurpees. Maybe we could hit some homemade hockey pucks and then rectify that situation. What do you think?"

I couldn't help laughing. Dad may be a rotten cook, but he was pretty good at cheering me up.

15

"You're doing it wrong!" I hovered next to Dad while he slathered peanut butter on a slice of bread. "You have to spread it evenly. See? That bite right there won't have any flavor, and this one will glue my mouth shut."

After a week of eating his sorry excuse for a peanut butter and jelly sandwich, I decided to offer pointers. Hadn't Mom told me I needed to pitch in more?

Dad slapped the jelly side onto the peanut butter side. Crooked. "It all goes to the same place, Annie. If you're so particular, perhaps you should make your own from now on." He stuck the sandwich in a bag with the already-made PB&J disaster and handed me my lunch.

"Mom always made it right." I spun around and stomped out of the kitchen.

"You're welcome!" Dad called.

I stuffed my lunch in my backpack, then marched to the door.

Dad had been doing everything wrong from the beginning. And trying to correct him didn't help, either. He just kept saying, "Well I'm not your mother." Duh, as if that wasn't painfully obvious.

"I'm going to Mrs. Schuster's," I announced.

Maybe Mrs. Schuster could do damage control on the sandwiches. After all, her secret rations had saved me more than once from being poisoned by Dad's awful cooking.

"Have a good day!" Dad yelled from the kitchen.

I waited a moment longer, but he didn't rush to the door like Mom did to insist on a hug and kiss. Again. Not that I liked that stuff. But routine was routine.

Another minute and I slipped out, swallowing back the lump in my throat that formed all too often these days.

Sloppy peanut butter and jelly sandwiches, burned dinners, and none of the little extras like a note in my lunch. And every day at lunch, Jessica and Jenny still asked me if I had a cookie or a hockey puck for dessert. Big mouth Lila.

I just wanted things back to the way they were.

At Mrs. Schuster's, I let myself in. The last time I knocked, I got a lecture. "Friends don't stand on formalities at my house. You know how to open a door, don't you?"

I pulled out the offending sandwiches and left my backpack in the entry. In the kitchen, Mrs. Schuster was frying eggs. I held up the baggies.

"We need some emergency medical attention here."

"Oh?"

"My dad just glops the peanut butter on and leaves the jelly in clumps." I'd never discussed the art of making peanut butter and jelly sandwiches with Mrs. Schuster, but it all seemed so obviously *wrong*, someone like Mrs. Schuster would surely understand.

Mrs. Schuster shook her head. "Amateur. Didn't spread it all the way to the edges, did he?"

I crossed my arms. "Not even close."

A quick spatula flick, and the eggs were on plates. Mrs. Schuster pulled a clean knife from the drawer. "It might not be too late if we hurry."

I put the sandwiches on the counter and held my breath as Mrs. Schuster performed sandwich surgery.

She pried the bread apart on the first and spread the peanut butter into an even layer that covered the *whole* slice. Using the knife, she massaged the jelly clumps till the purple side was smooth, the way it's supposed to be. Like a PB&J pro, she skimmed off the excess and flicked it into the sink.

"Better?" Mrs. Schuster let me inspect.

The peanut butter had purple flecks throughout, and the jelly had brown spots, but given the circumstances I could overlook it. I nodded my approval.

She did the same to the other sandwich, and I put them safely in my lunch bag. My shoulders felt lighter as I helped Mrs. Schuster carry our breakfasts to the table.

"So was Jason at soccer practice last night?" Mrs. Schuster asked.

I sat down with a thud. "No. That's two in a row now, not to mention the game. And since the note, he hasn't even acknowledged me at school. Kickball has been so boring I even agreed to play hopscotch with Lila and her drones yesterday."

They had all promised to cut the lunch jokes if I did. But it hadn't ended well, and I didn't want to talk about it. Lila had kept going on and on about some stupid shopping trip and some stupid expensive spa her mom was taking her to. When she started bragging about the expensive designer clothes she planned to get, I lost it.

"You are the most selfish person I know! Jason has to move because of money, and all you can do is brag about ways to waste it!"

I'd stomped off, but not before seeing the hurt look on Lila's face. Worse, I'd blabbed Jason's secret. I felt like total scum.

"But today's the last day of the punishment, right?" Mrs. Schuster swirled a finger in her pill cup. "Next week will be better."

I shook away the memory of what I'd done. "It can't be worse." I took a big bite of egg. "So what are you going to tell me about Black Marge today? I don't suppose *she* ever ate peanut butter and jelly sandwiches?"

Despite all the time I'd spent with Mrs. Schuster, I still hadn't gotten any more clues about the mystery. Jason would be disappointed. But after all the Black Marge stories, I was convinced she was real. Along with the treasure. I could tell by the look in Mrs. Schuster's eyes when she talked about it.

Definitely real.

Mrs. Schuster laughed. "That's where you'd be wrong. How do you think I learned to make them the right way?"

I squinted at her. "You're just making that up. They probably didn't even have peanut butter back then."

"So quick to doubt, are you?" She took a bite of yolk-dipped toast, chewing carefully before swallowing. "According to family history . . . and an entry in Black Marge's journal, my family may well be the originators of peanut butter."

"Now I *know* you're making it up."

Mrs. Schuster ignored me. "In her first journal entry after running away, Marge documented her getaway. Said she slipped out as soon as her old man's snoring reached its peak. She swiped a loaf of bread, the strawberry preserves their neighbor had brought over that morning, and her mammy's jar of protein paste."

"Protein paste?" I wrinkled my nose. "That sounds disgusting."

Mrs. Schuster laughed. "That's what they used to call peanut butter. Though it wasn't sweetened and processed. Just ground-up peanuts."

I still didn't believe her.

"After dumping out her papa's whiskey jar, she hightailed it out of town."

I took a swig of milk. "How old was she?"

"Fifteen. The first few days of her escape, she spread the preserves and the paste on the stale bread to soften it. First recorded peanut butter and jelly sandwich, right there. Not that I've done the research, but still, first *I've* ever heard of."

I couldn't help smiling. Maybe it wasn't so unbelievable. And it made sense that peanut butter and jelly sandwiches ran in Mrs. Schuster's family. That would explain why I liked her so much after only a couple of weeks. Good blood.

Mrs. Schuster cleared her throat. "I don't have proof, but family legend says Marge met up with a certain Dr. Kellogg on her way to California. Though Dr. Kellogg is often credited with inventing peanut butter, *we* know better."

"Cap'n Black Marge, the inventor of peanut butter." I grinned. I definitely didn't believe her, but it would be cool if peanut butter *did* have a secret history, so I played along. "Didn't she get *any* credit?"

"None. That same year, she met up with Lenny, later known as 'Leonard the Lout,' and with Marge posing as a boy, they joined the crew of a merchant ship. They didn't make it back to North America for years. Lenny really wasn't a lout in the beginning, you know. . . . I mean, according to Black Marge. She probably wouldn't have survived without him. He shared the little food he had, and then helped her find that job on the ship. It wasn't until they were captured by pirates that she saw his nasty side."

"So why didn't she just leave?"

"Leave? Didn't I just say she was captured? You don't just *leave* a pirate ship."

I blushed, because duh.

"No, Marge knew the only way she'd escape was by becoming feared. That was the period she was christened 'Black Marge.' And next thing she knew, she was made captain. And well, you know the rest."

I popped in my last bite of toast and wiped my hands on the linen napkin Mrs. Schuster insisted we use. "Wow, so Marge never even wanted to be a pirate, yet she managed to make off with all their treasure. Awesome!"

Mrs. Schuster cleared the dishes. "So what would you do if you found the treasure?"

Telling Mrs. Schuster was not the same thing as telling Lila. I decided to be honest. "I'm going to give it to Jason's dad so they can buy their house from the bank."

Mrs. Schuster paused, plate midair. She gave me a funny look. "That's . . . that's generous of you. But no shopping spree at the toy store? No fancy gadgets? No zombie-making cell phone?"

I laughed. "Well, maybe I'd splurge on that, but Jason comes first. He has to move if we can't get enough money to buy his house."

"And if you don't find it? Or . . . if there isn't a treasure?" Mrs. Schuster didn't look at me. She brushed a shaky hand at crumbs on the table.

I put on my brave face. True, some of my back-up plans hadn't worked out, but there was still my letter to Uncle Jim. Surely I could count on that.

But the question made me worry it wasn't enough. Maybe it was time to put Plan E in motion. "I've got back-up plans." I sat up straight and tried to sound confident. "We'll find a way for him to stay. We have to. I mean, my mom found a job like that." I snapped my fingers. "Maybe his dad will too. It's only fair."

I didn't mention our attempt to help with that. Between the radio contest and his reaction, I was too mad to talk about it.

The ceramic plates clinked as Mrs. Schuster walked toward the kitchen. "Life isn't always fair, my dear. You can't always get what you want. In fact, you probably won't. Just ask Marge." Her words sounded bitter. Harsh. Like the old Mrs. Schuster.

I heard the water run for a moment, then the protesting squeal of the dishwasher opening. Tears stung behind my eyes, but I let my anger push them back. I scowled at the kitchen, wishing I'd kept my mouth shut. I had thought Mrs. Schuster was different. That she believed in miracles, like I did. And what about all that talk about finding the good in the bad?

So what if life wasn't always fair? Did that mean you should sit back and not even try? Well I refused. I stood and walked stiffly to the kitchen. Mrs. Schuster stood at the sink. Her back was to me.

"I better go catch the bus. Thank you for breakfast."

"Wait." Mrs. Schuster turned. She stared at the floor and twisted a dish cloth in her hands. "I'm sorry. I — I shouldn't have said that."

I didn't say anything.

"Guess I've been too nice lately, and the grouchy lady in me wanted out."

I'm pretty sure she meant that as a joke. I didn't laugh.

She cleared her throat. "Truth is, I was being selfish. I've gotten kind of used to you coming around, and I was afraid you'd stop once the treasure thing gets sorted out . . . one way or the other. Since this rift between my son and me happened — and a few other things," she glanced at a pile of papers on the counter, "I've been more lonely than I care to admit."

My stomach flip-flopped. A clue! Something *had* happened, and those papers probably told the whole story.

"You are *completely* right to hope and work for the best. I really admire that about you. Can you forgive an old lady her skepticism? I'll try to be better. I promise."

Now it looked like Mrs. Schuster was about to cry. My heart melted. After all, she'd been an amazing friend. I didn't really want to lose her.

"Why wouldn't I come visit you after we find the treasure? You're my friend." I imagined burying a dead peanut butter and jelly sandwich with Mrs. Schuster in the garden. *She* would understand.

Mrs. Schuster sniffed. She wiped the dish towel over her eyes. "I've loved your visits. You're like the granddaughter I never had. But there's something else. Something I need to . . ."

A cuckoo clock sounded in the other room, and I jumped.

"The bus! I've gotta go."

With Mrs. Schuster trailing me, I ran to the door and grabbed my backpack. In that moment I had an idea. One I should have thought of sooner. "I have a soccer game at the middle school tomorrow. Ten o'clock if you want to come."

I felt shy inviting her after what had just happened, but the grin on Mrs. Schuster's face said it all.

16

The letter was on the entryway table when I got home from school. My heart *ka-thumped* as I stared at the return address: Mr. James A. Hill. Uncle Jim. This could fix everything. I *knew* he'd come through!

Clutching the letter, I ran upstairs.

"Hi, Dad." Without slowing down, I waved to him in the living room where he was reading the paper. "I'll do my homework in my room." I didn't wait for a response. At my parents' room, I paused long enough to poke my head in. "I'm home."

Mom mumbled something from the bed, like she had every day since she started the night shift. For once, I was glad. I barricaded myself in my room and ripped open the envelope: two typed pages, but no lottery tickets. I shook the envelope just to be sure. A butterfly tickled in my stomach till I came up with an explanation. Duh. Uncle Jim would have to claim the winnings for me. That made sense. I read the letter:

Dear Annie,

I thoroughly enjoyed your letter. You should write more often.

While I can appreciate your limited options given the circumstances, as the acknowledged money expert (please tell your mom "thanks" for the compliment), I cannot in good conscience spend your hard-earned money on lotto cards or Powerball numbers. Besides, your mother would kill me if she ever found out.

The butterflies were now a cement brick. Sitting. In the bottom of my stomach. I would have puked if bricks weren't so heavy. I couldn't believe Uncle Jim, Mr. I-eat-ice-cream-for-breakfast, was worried about my mom.

As an apology for the ill-suited gift I unwittingly sent for your last birthday, I have taken the liberty of adding to your savings. I'm doubling what you sent me.

Doubling was good. So why did I have such a bad feeling about this? Maybe because there was no money with the letter, either.

But wait, there's more. What could be better than more money, you ask? I have taken the liberty of investing your money in one of my favorite dividend-yielding stocks.

Huh?

I have set it to reinvest the dividends so by the time you go to college, you'll have a substantial sum. I don't know why I didn't think of this before. The perfect gift for any age. And now I won't have to stress about birthdays and Christmas. I'll just add to it.

No need to thank me. Though I'd always enjoy another letter.

Sincerely,
Uncle Jim

P.S. You can expect to receive your stock certificates in the mail in a few weeks.

I read the letter several times before crumpling the thing. "What the heck is a dividend-yielding stock?" I moaned. "And what part of 'buy as many lottery tickets as you can' didn't he understand?!"

Not only did it sting that my uncle blatantly refused to help me, but I was shocked he would rob me blind. And I couldn't even complain to Mom!

I hurled the wad of paper at the trash can and flopped onto my bed. I'd have to start saving for an iPhone all over again! Rotten uncle.

Now I knew why Uncle Jim let us have ice cream for breakfast — he was clueless.

I stared at the ceiling. Plan A hadn't worked out, Plan B was iffy at best, Plan C had been a pointless waste of time, and Plan D went beyond failure into the realm of catastrophe.

There was no other choice. I had to use Plan E. Jason wouldn't like it, and neither would our parents, but Mrs. Schuster was right. What if we didn't find the treasure? Or it turned out to be worthless? Or worse, it didn't exist? I couldn't take that chance, because based on the last two weeks, I simply couldn't survive without Jason.

17

When I woke up the next day, I bolted out of bed. Today was the day. The end of being grounded. I didn't care I was still in pajamas, I wanted to head to Jason's house right then. But yesterday Mom had laid down the law before her stupid night shift.

"You two aren't officially ungrounded until your soccer game. No sunrise visits."

"Will you be there?" I'd asked.

Mom shook her head. "I'm sorry, kiddo. After working all night, I need to get some sleep before my next shift."

Of course she did. Because sleep is more important than her own daughter.

I just nodded and pretended I understood.

It wasn't like she'd abandoned me, or whatever. She just had to work. A lot.

Never mind that she missed last week's game too. But I wasn't going to think about that. Not today. Today was about Jason.

By the time nine-thirty came around, I'd eaten breakfast, cleaned my room, watered the plants, taken out the trash, practiced the piano, and caught an episode of some random Japanese anime. The game was at ten and it only took five minutes to walk to the middle school, but I didn't care. I was ready to leap out of my skin. I couldn't wait another second.

"Come on, Dad! Let's go!"

Dad laughed. "Just hold on. Matt, Kate, are you sure you won't come?"

"We're sure," they called from downstairs. The TV blared in the background.

"We could kick the ball around. All four of us. And the traditional Slurpees afterward."

I held my breath. *Please don't let them come,* I prayed.

"Not interested," Kate called.

"Ditto, that," Matt said.

"Amen!" I said. "Let's go!" Ball in hand, I clacked down the stairs in my cleats. I really liked that sound. The sound of game day. I clomped down the driveway as noisily as I could until my dad finally caught up.

He pushed his glasses back in place. "Think you'll end your losing streak today?"

I tossed my ball in the air. "It's not a losing streak. We could totally win if we chose. We just don't want to destroy the other kids' morale."

"I see. Very generous of you."

"Besides, winning isn't worth the brutality. Some kids take this stuff pretty seriously. But I mean, geez. The ref doesn't even keep score."

Dad pushed his glasses back up. Again. "You're a pretty good kid. You know that?"

"Da-ad!" I looked around to make sure no one had heard. The last thing I needed was to get a reputation as the "good kid."

Since he started staying home, Dad was always saying things like that. I didn't mind so much at the house, but I was going to have to be more careful about taking him out in public. I debated the idea of training him on acceptable things to say, but I doubted he'd take me seriously.

At the corner, I glanced at Jason's house. No sign of him. It took all my will power not to go knock on his door to see if he wanted to walk together. But I didn't want to muff anything up before we were officially ungrounded.

With a sigh, I crossed the street and headed the opposite direction toward the middle school. I needed to distract myself. I glanced at Dad, who whistled "Yankee Doodle" out of key. Nothing like a second trauma to distract me from the first.

"So, any luck with the job hunt? That's why you're always reading the paper, isn't it? I bet you'll have a job in no time." I tried to sound casual. I didn't want him to think I didn't want him around. I did. I just *preferred* Mom.

"I read the paper to stay informed," Dad said, and there went those glasses again. He should really find a way to keep them up better.

"Your mother and I have decided that I won't look for a job yet. She misses you, of course, but she's enjoying her work. And you kids are important to us. We can't let just anybody take care of you."

"So you're *not* getting a job?" I hoped I'd misunderstood.

Dad laughed. "Yep, you're stuck with me. Think you can handle that?"

My knees trembled. Not that I didn't love my dad. He was good for some things — like practicing soccer or going out for Slurpees — but no way he could replace Mom. I'd thought this whole thing was temporary. Until he found a job.

I kicked a pebble into the street, where a passing car zoomed over it. Why couldn't things go back the way they were? Back before my dad was laid off. Heck, before Jason's house was for sale.

But when I thought of Jason I felt ashamed. His situation was tons worse. Neither his mom *nor* dad had a job. And he was going to have to move.

I should have felt lucky. I didn't.

But I was Annie Jenkins, super spy, master of deception. I could fake it.

Ignoring the knot in my stomach, I squinted at my dad. "Well . . . I guess so. But I might have to put you on probation if you keep burning the toast." I even managed a wink.

Dad grinned and wiped at his forehead. "Phew! For a second I thought you were going to say 'no.' Never you fear, I'll figure out that toaster. I mean, I have an MBA and everything. Toast should be a snap."

I looked away. 'Cause two weeks of burned toast didn't give a girl confidence.

Dad cleared his throat, and when I looked back, he'd gone all serious on me. "I want you to know that our decision is about more than burned toast. I had these three amazing children who were growing up to be wonderful young adults thanks to your mother, but I rarely ever got to see you. Just weekends, and sometimes not even then. I wasn't okay with that. So I guess you could say that my layoff was an opportunity. One I couldn't pass up."

I'd never thought about how my dad felt. He went to work and came home. That's the way it had always been. It never occurred to me that he might not be happy.

I slipped my hand into his and we walked the rest of the way in silence. The comfortable kind that felt like a blanket. Maybe it wouldn't be so bad to have Dad stay home.

At the field, we kicked the ball around while we waited for the rest of my team. When Lila got there I thought she'd try to butt in on our practice, like usual, but she didn't even look our direction. Weird.

Then Mrs. Schuster got there. Dad ran to carry the camping chair she'd brought. I ran and gave her a hug.

"I can't believe you came!"

"Of course I came. In my day, invitations were neither given nor received lightly. I hope you score a home run for your team."

I snorted back a laugh. "You mean kick a goal."

"Whatever." Mrs. Schuster tapped Dad's arm and pointed to the ground. "This will do fine, young man."

While Dad set up the chair, she leaned in close. "So we're good about yesterday? You forgive me?"

I nodded and Mrs. Schuster stamped her cane. She gave a curt nod, then settled into her chair. "Go kick some booty, as you kids would probably say."

By the time Jason arrived, the team was huddled around the coach, the game about to start. The other players started whispering, but my attention was on my friend. I grinned so wide I thought my face would crack. Until I noticed his dad standing there.

In Sunday school they say you're not supposed to hate people, but I was having a hard time with Mr. Parker.

"Ted, it's great to see you!" My dad shook Mr. Parker's hand, so I took the liberty of sending Mr. Parker the dirty look he deserved before waving Jason over.

He squished into the circle next to me. The whispering got louder.

"I thought today would never come," he said under his breath.

"Mr. Parker, welcome!" the coach boomed. "Just in time. Now quiet down everybody. What did we learn in practice? First . . ."

I eyed the bandage on Jason's knee while the team droned the answers to his questions.

Jason whispered in my ear. "Mom made me bandage it for the game. You know, all that slide tackling we do." He rolled his eyes. "So did you find any more clues?"

"Affirmative. Plus I . . ."

"Annie! Jason! Are you two listening?"

I caught Lila staring at us from the other side of the circle, and she hurriedly looked away. I'd have bet the cemetery she'd told on us.

Jason and I nodded enthusiastically. Fake smile in place, I kept my eyes on the coach to make it look like I was paying attention.

When he started drawing plays on his whiteboard, I glanced at Lila. She wasn't Miss Perky today. At all. Her eyes had dark circles under them like she hadn't slept. And I doubted she was listening to the coach either. Still, she'd already told on us once. I think.

I scootched closer to Jason. "I'll tell you later."

It was probably for the best. Between Plan E, the treasure, and the clue, I had a lot to tell him.

"Go Penguins, on the count of three!" The coach put his hand in the center of the circle.

We stuck our arms in with the rest of the team. "Go Penguins!"

I heard the other team guffawing and I blushed for the billionth time at our stupid team name. Lila had been on a penguin kick the first week of practice, and Lila always got her way. As if being cute and blond meant anything in soccer. Thank heavens Jess and Jen weren't on the team, too. I might have had to quit.

"Annie?" Lila blocked my way to the field. She glanced at Jason, who stood next to me. "I just wanted to say . . ." Another look at Jason. "I mean, I'm sorry. I didn't know."

When I didn't say anything, she hung her head. "Just. Sorry." She ran off to take her position.

"What was that all about?" Jason asked.

My face burned red. I couldn't tell him I'd blabbed his secret. Luckily Coach Reed saved me.

"Jenkins! Pick it up. You're up front, center-left. Parker, you're here with me. Let's go, let's go!" The coach hustled me onto the field, clamping a hand on Jason's shoulder.

As I ran on the field, I heard Jason's dad. "You dragged me out here so I could watch you ride the bench? Of all the . . ."

I wanted to smack him across the head. Mr. Parker was the one who deserved to be grounded.

When the whistle blew to start the game, I struggled to get into it. The ball flew past me, followed by two opposing players. I doubt my team had even moved when the ball swooshed into our goal.

I groaned. Business as usual. It would be another painful forty minutes for all involved. Except the other team, of course. They were smiling and high-fiving like they'd actually *done something* to get that goal.

By the end of the first half, the score was seven to zero. Though my dad cheered us on, Jason's dad stood by himself, his thumbs jabbing at his phone.

Last spring he'd been our biggest supporter — cheering us on even when we were behind by twenty. (That only happened once. Really.) Now, he didn't even look up when the whistle blew to start the second half.

This time, Jason and I were forwards together. It was our kick-off. We had practiced for just such a moment. We had a plan. "You ready?" I asked.

Jason nodded.

I tapped the ball to him and ran as hard as I could to get into position, just wide of the last player. Jason was supposed to kick it to me, but when I turned, he'd long since lost the ball.

Three goals later, with maybe five minutes left in the game, a miracle finally happened. Bryce, the biggest and least coordinated kid on the team, managed to clear the ball. About time!

Everyone gaped as it soared through the sky. Except me and Jason.

We dashed upfield past the opposing defenders who hadn't bothered to stay in position. I got there first, dribbling past midfield. Jason broke wide, "accidentally" getting in the way of the defenders behind us.

With only the goalie left to defend the net, I wanted to celebrate. Five years of practice would finally pay off. Because till now, I'd never even scored a goal. Actually, no one on my team had (at least for our own team). I'd be the first! I could already feel my teammates lifting me onto their shoulders.

Out of the corner of my eye, I caught a glimpse of Jason. He ran parallel to me on the opposite side of the field. He was wide open.

Then I remembered. He'd never scored either.

The defenders were riding my back. Their hot breath sent goose bumps up my arms. The goalie rushed at me. I needed to shoot. Now.

I aimed and kicked.

The goalie dove. The defenders slid from behind, knocking me over. Totally illegal! But the ball whizzed past them, right to Jason.

Without even breaking stride, he shot the ball. I held my breath, but I shouldn't have worried. The ball swished into the upper corner of the goal.

The crowd erupted as the whistle blew to end the game.

Jason ran straight to me and pulled me to my feet. "We did it! We scored! We scored!"

We jumped up and down, celebrating. "We scored! We scored! We scored!"

"What dweebs." The other team's goalie sneered at us. "The score's ten to one . . . for us."

Jason and I paused.

"You lost." The goalie snorted, then launched a gob of green onto the field.

We stared at him a moment, then continued our celebration. "We scored! We scored!" Our team mobbed us and joined in the dance.

I caught a glimpse of Lila watching from the other side of the field, then Bryce smashed into our mob of teammates and I forgot about her.

"On our shoulders!" Bryce shouted.

Jason and I laughed the whole way as our teammates half-carried, half-dragged us to our coach. We gave a cheer, shook the other team's hands, then ran straight for our dads. I couldn't wait to see the look on Mr. Parker's face.

"Did you see that?" Jason glowed.

Warmth filled my chest. Jason hadn't looked so happy in months! I'd made the right choice by passing to him.

"Great assist, Annie! And awesome goal, Jason! You two make a great team!" My dad scooped me into a hug.

"Wonderful, you two! Just wonderful." Mrs. Schuster beamed at us. "That last five minutes made up for the other miserable thirty-five." I couldn't help giving her a hug, because amen to that!

"Did you see that, Dad? Wasn't it great?" Jason stood in front of his father.

I waited for the reaction. The smile. The high-fives and knuckle punch. The congratulations and proud words. Maybe even a hug.

Jason's dad looked up from his phone. "Is the game over? Good, I've got a lot to get done at home, and . . ."

"But my goal." Jason pointed at the net as though his dad could watch the instant replay. "Didn't you see it? I scored!"

His dad was back at his phone. "You scored?" He sounded distracted. "Cool. Now let's go. Nice to see you, Sam." With a glance our direction, he started walking toward home.

I stood there stunned. We all did. We'd gone five years without a single goal, and all he could say was '"cool"?! Couldn't he at least have faked a smidgen of enthusiasm? Maybe act like he cared? This was a big deal — our moment of triumph. And he'd ruined it.

My dad finally broke the silence. "Well I'm proud of both of you. Slurpees on me. Ted, do you mind if Jason comes?" he called.

Mr. Parker waved a hand, not looking up or stopping.

Jason watched his dad walk away. I flinched at each step.

"I don't really feel like celebrating." He wouldn't look at me.

"But what about our Slurpee contest?"

"Guess I forfeit." He shuffled toward his dad.

"But . . ." I felt helpless. I wanted to fix things. Make them right for Jason. But I couldn't. He needed his dad for that — the old one. Just like I needed my mom. Like peanut butter needed jelly.

Why did things have to change? Everything had been perfect, and now we were all miserable.

I wondered if the treasure would be enough to bring back the old Mr. Parker. The fun one who could make Jason laugh without trying. Hopefully we'd find out soon now that we weren't grounded anymore.

"I'll come over after lunch?" I asked.

Jason shrugged, not stopping. "Whatever."

18

After lunch I ran straight to Jason's.

"He's up cleaning his room," Mrs. Parker said. "You can help him if you want, but after that you two will have to play elsewhere. We have a showing in thirty minutes."

I struggled not to scowl as she led me upstairs. My stomach cramped when we passed the family room. The TV and couch set were already gone, making the room look the way I felt: empty. But by the time we got to Jason's room, I had an idea.

Jason was picking up Legos in the corner. I nonchalantly joined him. "So," I said. "Your mom told me about the showing. What if we . . ."

"No."

"It wouldn't have to . . ."

"No." Jason kept cleaning. "No sabotage."

"Fine." I sighed.

We worked together in silence until his room was clean, then trudged downstairs to report to his mom. When she okayed his room, I dragged Jason to the cemetery and told him to wait.

His eyes nearly bugged out of his head when I returned with the bulging sack.

"Whoa! What happened?"

I laid the thirteen sandwiches in a row. "Two from the vacant lot fiasco, and the rest are from school lunch."

Jason blinked. "Wait. Were those the ones for me? You kept bringing them?"

"All but one. Lila made me so mad that first day, I couldn't eat. Anyway, I had to keep bringing them. Just in case. Society members keep their word. Remember?"

He sat up straighter. Grinned. "So thirteen burials, huh? We'd better get started."

"Actually I had an idea. We could . . ." I clamped a hand over my mouth.

"What's wrong?"

I shook my head. Took a deep breath. I'd planned this all out, and had even practiced what to say. It had to be official. "I can't tell you until I start the meeting."

Jason rolled his eyes. "Then start it already, you goof."

I cleared my throat. "I hereby call this meeting of the PB&J Society to order. Before we begin, I'd like to propose the addition of two new rules to be hereafter known as Rule Number Seven and Rule Number Eight.

"If approved, Rule Number Seven shall be written as follows: 'No SPB&J burials shall take place unless both Society members are present.' Rule Number Eight . . ."

"What?" Jason sat up straight. "You held a ceremony without me, didn't you?"

I shook my head. "I tried, but it wasn't the same. That's why we need a rule."

"Then aye. But it shouldn't have to be a rule."

I squirmed. Studied the row of sandwiches. "I haven't called for the vote yet," I finally said. I finally looked up. "I also propose Rule Number Eight which, if approved, shall be written in the books as follows: 'If more than three PB&Js require burial at the same time, a mass burial shall be performed. Instead of holding each sandwich to spit upon, thou shalt line them up on the ground, and both members shall perform a rapid-fire spit salute (one spit for each sandwich).'

"All in favor, say 'aye.'"

Jason squinted at me. Shook his head. "Aye."

I added mine.

"All opposed, say 'nay.'" I scanned the crowds, then gave a nod. "It's unanimous. The 'ayes' have it. Let the ceremony begin."

I reached for a sandwich to inspect, but Jason raised his hand again. "Time-out."

"What?"

"So how do we do this? You only mentioned the spitting, but who inspects? Or do we both inspect? And do we do it one sandwich at a time, or both together? Rule Number Eight isn't very clear."

My hands were at my hips. "Then you should have said something *before* you voted for it. You had no problem commenting on Rule Number Seven."

"I was in a hurry to approve Seven before you held another ceremony without me." Jason winked.

He wasn't mad! Laughter bubbled up inside me, but I bit it back. This was the ceremony. This was serious business. But man I'd missed him! "Okay, okay. How about we take turns inspecting the sandwiches and do it one at a time. And then we'll both dig the hole. I even brought two shovels. Acceptable?"

"Acceptable. Time-in."

I picked up the first, turned it frontward and backward, then rotated it to check the sides. "I hereby pronounce this sandwich mold-free and worthy of burial."

Jason inspected the second, and we continued back and forth until he picked up the twelfth. It was the smushed flat one from the vacant lot. "Eww gross! I hereby pronounce this sandwich moldy and unfit for burial." He held it pinched between two fingers so I could see the green on the corner.

I shivered, snatched up the bag I'd brought them in and held it out. He deposited it inside and I set the thing as far from me as I could.

The last sandwich wasn't as smushed, but it was from that same day. Bracing myself for grossness, I picked it up, inspected, and phew. "I hereby pronounce this sandwich mold-free and worthy of burial."

I laid it back in line, and we started digging. The ground was hard, and we were both sweating by the time the hole was big enough. But I loved working side by side with Jason. For a moment I forgot about the looming black cloud.

We kneeled on either side of the PB&J line.

"Let the rapid-fire spitting begin!" I hadn't told Jason about the addition, but he didn't seem to care. He just started spitting.

Ptooey! Ptooey!

I spit with all my might, imagining I was hitting the wretched moving sign. I didn't stop until Jason tapped me.

"Time-out. Wasn't it only one spit per sandwich?"

I wiped the spit droplets from my face. "Oh. Guess I forgot to count. Sorry."

He nodded. "Time-in."

Trying not to touch the spitty parts, we took turns laying the sandwiches in the hole, then placed our hands on our stomachs.

"Our dearly beloveds, we are gathered here today to say goodbye to these sandwiches. We are saddened by the loss of our favorite food and think on happier times before they were smushed and became gross. We are grateful for the many times they saved us from the evils of broccoli casserole and bid them farewell on their new journey to feed the worms. May they rest in peace."

When the song was sung, and the hole filled, we went inside to wash our hands, then sat down on the back steps to eat the popsicles my dad had given us.

With red juice slipping down my chin, I eyed the Parkers' turkey pen. I needed to tell Jason about the treasure. Five measly steps! Why did Black Marge choose an obvious number like 100? She should have been tricky and chosen 87 or 62. Anything but 100! (Well, and preferably not 96, 97, 98, or 99 either.)

I couldn't remember the last time I'd been in Jason's backyard. The turkey pen took up half of it, and I didn't trust the wire fence that separated the birds from the grass. In my book, Jason's backyard was akin to broccoli casserole: to be avoided at all costs. But with the treasure on the line, I'd have to make an exception.

When the last bit of my popsicle fell on the steps, I took a deep breath. Time to tell Jason what I'd found. I just hoped his mood didn't nosedive when I mentioned the treasure.

"So I found a clue yesterday."

Jason paused from sucking on the last bit of his popsicle. "Yeah?"

"Mrs. Schuster was talking about that fight with her son, then she told me that other bad stuff was going on too. She looked right at a pile of papers when she said it. Whatever she's hiding, it's there. I'm sure of it."

"Really? What do you think they say?"

"I don't know. I wasn't close enough to read them."

"We need a plan." Jason tapped his stick on the stair.

I shifted to face him. "It's simple. You spill your milk, and I'll run to the kitchen for some napkins. If the papers are there I'll find out what they say."

Jason snorted. "First, when has Mrs. Schuster ever let us help do anything? Never. That's when. And second, even if she did let you help, don't you think she'd notice if you took too long? You know how she is about cleaning."

I slumped. "Oh. Right."

We sat there trying to think of a plan, but short of breaking and entering, I had nothing.

"Well," I finally said, "we aren't expert spies for nothing. One of these mornings she'll make a mistake. They always do. And we'll be ready."

Jason laughed. "You're such a kook."

"Speaking of that . . ." My hands suddenly felt clammy. Jason was going to laugh (either that or get mad), but I needed him to believe me.

"Uh-oh."

"I think the treasure's real."

"Annie, we've been through this." His voice went tired.

"You should have heard her, Jason. Mrs. Schuster wasn't just telling me all kinds of stories about Black Marge. She talked about it like it was real. Like she was there or something. Plus Black Marge kept a journal."

"You saw it?"

"No." Right then I wished I'd pushed the issue a little harder. "But she left clues about the treasure in it."

Jason didn't say anything. He stared at his feet.

"I think it's in your backyard."

He raised his eyebrows

"The treasure's here. I'm sure of it." I told him about the clues: the pear trees; the one hundred steps. I told him about my failed attempt to reach the treasure.

I could tell he wanted to believe.

"Five steps from the fence," I said.

We both stared at the pen. I couldn't take my eyes off the strutting birds.

Jason finally shook his head. "So you're saying you'd face turkeys for this pretend treasure?"

"Isn't your dad selling them?" I squirmed. Because as much as I wanted to dig up the treasure, I couldn't go in there with a turkey on the loose. I just couldn't.

"Next week," Jason said.

My insides giggled, I was so happy at the news.

Look. Real or not, my dad'll kill us if we dig a big hole in there." He glanced at his house. "Maybe . . . I mean, it might be time to give up. My dad *still* grumbles about that trip to the doctor. He freaks out at the smallest things now. I don't think any treasure is worth the risk of upsetting him. Especially a made-up one."

"Jason." My mom poked her head out the back door. "Your mom called. You can go home whenever you like."

"Thanks, Mrs. Jenkins."

I looked away. My nose tingled in that I'm-about-to-cry way. I tried to picture my future without Jason, but I could only see black. I couldn't let him give up.

If he refused to search for the treasure, then it was time for Plan E.

Jason stood to go in, but I jumped in front of him. "There's one more possibility."

"Yeah?" Jason spoke hesitantly.

"We talk to the bank."

"What!? No way. If you thought two weeks was bad, it'll seem like nothing after our punishment for that. Besides, we don't even know what bank to visit."

"So find out. You know where your parents keep stuff, don't you? Do a little research."

"You mean snooping."

"Research," I repeated. "And no one has to know what we're doing. We'll just say we're going on a bike ride. And that will be the truth. Thankfully, Dad made Matt fix my bike."

"Right."

I ignored Jason's sarcasm. "Monday is a short day. We'll go right after school so we have more time. Can you get the info by then?"

Jason closed his eyes, then laughed. "You are crazy, Annie. Fine, I'm in. But only because you'd go bug every bank in town otherwise."

I stuck out my hand. "Peanut butter," I said, and grinned when Jason added his 'Jelly.' There was no going back after the handshake.

19

By Monday morning, Jason had found what we needed. We talked plans on the way to the bus stop after breakfast at Mrs. Schuster's. He even seemed excited.

"It's First Regional Bank of Northern Utah. They have a branch on Main Street."

"That'll be a long ride, but definitely doable," I said. "And I've been thinking about what to say all weekend. If you . . ."

"Why are they all looking at me like that?" Jason paused. We were across the street from the bus stop.

I followed his gaze. A first grader smiled and waved, but most didn't look like they'd even noticed us.

"Well they were," Jason said.

I elbowed him. "You're just being paranoid about our 'bike ride' this afternoon."

"I know what I saw."

As we stepped in line, the bus pulled up. A third grader in front of us glanced back. When she saw us notice, her face turned red and she jerked her head to face forward.

"See?" Jason whispered.

I frowned. "Maybe they saw us come out of Mrs. Schuster's house."

When we climbed on, the bus went silent followed by furious whispering.

Had we missed some inside joke or something? The whispers got louder as we passed each row.

It was a relief to sit down and pretend everything was normal. But when the same thing happened in our classroom, I started to get nervous.

Jessica and Jenny huddled around Lila at her cubby. Jason went to hang up his backpack, and the twins giggled madly.

"Stop it, you guys." Lila's cheeks were pink and she wouldn't look at us.

In fact, she wouldn't look at me the whole morning. Which was perfectly okay with me. Even better, she didn't sit with us at lunch.

I decided that whatever was going on was a good thing. I held up my milk carton to Jason. "Cheers to a peaceful lunch!"

Jason bumped his carton against mine, but before we could drink, Jessica . . . or maybe it was Jenny . . . went and opened her big mouth.

"Hey, Jason! We'll pay you a dollar to clear our trays for us. Annie tells us you need the money!" They cackled like the evil witches they were and dropped four quarters on the table.

The cafeteria was silent listening to those quarters spin to a stop. A couple of laughs broke out, then the place erupted in too-loud whispering.

The cafeteria aides rushed to the tables, yelling something at us, but my face burned so hot, all I could hear was static.

Jason was red, too. He carefully placed his milk in the corner of his tray. "Annie?" He looked at me, eyes pleading. "She's lying. I mean, she has to be, right? Because you wouldn't . . ."

I shook my head. "No, I . . . I mean, not on purpose . . . not like . . ." I couldn't finish. There was no excuse for betraying your best friend.

Jason stood abruptly, knocking the table. He grabbed his tray and his milk carton tipped, milk glogging everywhere as he fled.

I grabbed my stuff and ran after him. "Jason, wait!"

He dumped his tray into the garbage can and headed for the exit.

"Please! I'm sorry. It was an accident! I didn't mean to tell. It's just that Lila was going on about . . ."

Jason spun around and I almost ran into him. "Everything's an accident with you, Annie. What I told you was private. You had no right to tell. No right!"

He stormed away, but this time I didn't follow. I found a vacant wall to curl up against until it was time to go in.

I know Mrs. Starry said stuff the rest of the afternoon, but I didn't hear any of it. I laid my head on my desk and kept replaying that moment with Lila, wishing I could change the past by remembering it differently. I needed to make this right.

When the final bell rang, Jason was first out the door. I rushed after him, but Lila blocked me. "I told them not to do it. Jessica and Jenny can be really dumb sometimes."

"Whatever." Lila was the last person I wanted to talk to. Okay, maybe Jessica and Jenny were last, but close enough. I pushed past her and raced down the hall to catch Jason. The hall monitor sent me back. Twice.

By the time I got on the bus, the seat next to Jason was filled.

"Jason." I waited for him to say something. He didn't. "I'm sorry."

He just stared out the window.

The bus door wooshed shut and the driver eyed me in his enormous mirror. "Find a seat, please."

The only place left was with a first grader up front, but I didn't care. At least I'd beat Jason off the bus. Because after two weeks without him, I wasn't above begging. On my knees if I had to.

When we got to our stop, I hovered next to Jason the moment he stepped off. As soon as we crossed the street I bombarded him with explanation.

"We were playing hopscotch and Li—"

I caught Lila watching us. She looked so sad I hesitated.

". . . and Jessica and Jenny were going on about designer clothes and blah, blah, blah, and I exploded at how wasteful they were when — when *others* were in need."

"Others?" Jason snapped. "You mean me."

I nodded, just glad he was talking to me.

He hitched up his backpack and walked faster.

"I'm really sorry! What do you want me to say? I can't change what happened."

He finally stopped and faced me. We were at the cul-de-sac. "You just don't get it! You act like this is all some big game, but it's not. Do you have any idea how it feels to know you could be kicked out of your house any day? To have your dad suddenly turn into this stranger?

"Well I'll tell you. It stinks! And now on top of that I have to deal with everybody staring at me like I'm some charity case. Well I'm not. My family works hard and we're just as good as everyone else!"

I felt like scum. I was supposed to be getting rid of Jason's worries, not adding more. I kicked at a pebble. "I think you're better. I really am sorry."

Jason was silent, but he didn't leave. Did that mean he didn't hate me? I clung to that hope and cleared my throat. "So. What about our plans?"

Jason closed his eyes.

I took a deep breath. "Please. I know this isn't a game. If you move I . . ." My throat closed. I couldn't even think about the possibility.

"Fine." Jason sighed. "Meet me here in ten minutes. But only because we shook on it. I'm still mad at you."

I was there in five.

When Jason showed, his frown kept me from jumping with glee.

"You MapQuested it?" I asked.

I couldn't keep the surprise off my face when he held out a hand-drawn map.

His cheeks flashed pink and he fiddled with his handbrake. "The internet was down so I used the yellow pages."

The what pages? I bit my lip and nodded. "We won't get lost, right?"

Jason's mouth tightened. "It's easy to get there. We'll be fine. But if you're worried, maybe we shouldn't go."

I took the sheet from him and studied the directions. "A half-hour, you think?"

We headed down the street in silence. I let Jason lead since he knew the way. At first I used the time to think about what I'd say, but the thought of facing a stuffed-shirt banker was making me nervous. Better not to think about it.

When we reached the bank, we chained our bikes to a tree near the entrance.

"I'll do the talking?" I said.

I took Jason's silence as agreement.

We pushed through the doors and stood staring at the richly decorated lobby. The crystal chandelier that hung in the center of the room reminded me of *Beauty and the Beast*. It reflected a group of jiggling rainbows on the fancy patterned carpet. Rainbows were a good sign.

To our right, several tellers stood behind a wood-paneled counter. One smiled at me, while another tapped furiously at his keyboard. A third worked with a customer, though a tall sandy-haired man in a dark blue suit stood over her shoulder giving directions.

I felt bad for that teller because the man looked mean. I decided it was the beard. Sure Santa has one, but he's about the only guy I know who could get away with that. Besides, Santa's is big and fluffy and white. This guy's was close-trimmed and darkish.

"Can I help you?"

A pretty blonde smiled at us from behind a desk. Besides hers, there was a whole row of desks with fancy chairs, though they were all empty. I hoped that didn't mean they'd had to fire a bunch of people.

When neither of us spoke, the woman continued. "Do you want to open accounts? You'll need your parents to do it, but I can send some information home with you."

Jason elbowed me.

I stepped forward. "Um, we wanted to talk to someone about a loan."

The woman shook her head. "I'm afraid banks don't loan money to . . ."

"Oh, we don't want to *get* a loan. We already have one . . . well, his parents do. We just want to talk to someone in charge."

The woman's eyebrows shot up, though her smile never faded. "I see. Sounds like you need to speak with Mr. Lightner. Unfortunately, he doesn't come in on Mondays." She motioned toward an office beyond the desks.

Before the disappointment could sink in, a man cleared his throat behind us. "May I be of service?"

"Sir! I . . ." The woman started to stand, but the man waved her back down.

"I'll just borrow Mr. Lightner's office and help these future customers myself."

I swallowed. It was the mean-looking, bearded man.

"Right this way."

I glanced at Jason, but he wouldn't look at me.

The man ushered us into an office and gestured to some cushy chairs.

From the other side of a large desk, the man folded his arms and leaned forward to rest on them. He threw out one of those fake smiles adults always make for kids. "If we were in my own office, I'd offer you both a sucker. Unfortunately, my office is in the city. I hope you'll forgive me."

Just how young did he think we were? Suckers were for babies. Still, we needed his help, so I curbed my sarcasm. "That's okay, sir. Our parents don't let us accept candy from strangers, anyway."

The man cleared his throat. "Yes. Well. Very wise of them. You should definitely listen to your parents. So. How may I help you two today? I heard something about a loan? If I had to guess, I'd say you two are getting married and need a loan for your first home."

He chuckled at his own joke, laughing harder when Jason leaned away from me.

I went from horrified to angry. Did he think he was funny? How dare this stranger tease us about ma— I couldn't even *think* the word. If he were in our class, I'd punch him in the nose, school policy or not. If it were Matt or Kate, I'd tell on him.

Adults always think the rules don't apply to them. And this man worked in a bank, for cripes sake. He should know better. Well, he was going down.

No ring on his left hand.

I had a plan.

Straightening up, I reached over to pat Jason's shoulder. I tried not to feel hurt when he flinched. "How did you know? We've been best friends so long, it just seemed like the next step to take."

I ignored the look of disgust on Jason's face and poured a syrup smile for the man. "I see *you're* not wearing a ring. If you ever need advice, we're like experts. All the fifth graders come to us for help, and we'd be more than happy to help you, too."

The man stopped laughing and turned a bright shade of pink. I didn't flinch. Not even when Jason kicked me.

"I . . . uh . . . I'll have to remember that." The man pulled at his collar. "My mother didn't send you, did she?"

I folded my arms and gave him the look. That'd teach him to mess with me.

I didn't expect him to start laughing again. And I especially didn't expect him to look *nice* when he lost the fake smile.

"Okay," the man conceded, "you are most right. I shouldn't tease like that. My mother would be appalled. But you two looked like you had a great sense of humor so I took a chance. I'm terribly sorry to have offended you."

His eyes twinkled in a familiar way. Like my dad's? I squinted at him, suddenly sure I'd seen him before, but I couldn't think where.

Jason elbowed me and I realized the man was waiting to shake hands. I gripped his hand firmly. "Apology accepted."

After he shook Jason's hand, too, I got down to business. "We came to talk about his parents' loan."

The man studied Jason, who shrunk back into his chair. "I see. Well I'm sorry you came all this way, but bank policy says I can only speak about a loan with the loan holder. If your parents would like to come in themselves, I'd be happy to talk to them."

Jason nodded, looking miserable. His hands clutched the arms of his chair in a death grip.

"We don't want to talk *about* the loan," I said. "We already know enough. We know you want to take away their house."

Jason stared at the ground.

The man's lips tightened.

"We don't need details. We just came to ask you not to take their house away. Please." Adults like it when kids use polite junk like that.

The man sat back and took a deep breath. "I can see how this must look from your perspective. Believe it or not, the bank doesn't want your parents' house." He spoke to Jason. "The bank only repossesses a home after a loan holder fails to pay their loan several months in a row."

"His dad lost his job," I blurted. "He's a hard worker. He'll get another job, and then he'll pay. He will. We're just asking you to give him a break. His name's Ted Parker."

Silence filled the room. I didn't break my gaze until he spoke. "I'm sure this sounds harsh to you, but if the bank did that for everyone who failed to pay, we'd go out of business. And without going into details, the consequences would be much worse. For more than just your family."

I was about to argue, but Jason jumped to his feet. "Don't waste your breath, Annie. He's not going to help us. Let's go."

I shook my head at the man the way my mom always does when she's disappointed in me. I hoped he felt as bad as I always did.

What a waste. For a second, I'd thought the man could solve our problems. But bankers were just as stuffy as I'd imagined.

We rode home in silence. I didn't want to admit we were running out of options, but the truth was getting harder and harder to ignore.

Jason would have to move if we didn't come up with something quick.

I thought of the list. Maybe Hollywood was the answer. Or begging somewhere in the city might get us the money faster.

"Great." Jason slowed down and I nearly ran into him.

I squeezed the brake and swerved, coming to a stop. My relief was short lived. A congregation of adults stood on the street corner between our houses.

I groaned. This probably meant that sneaking away to beg wouldn't work out either.

My mom pushed her way through the crowd. She wore scrubs, and she had her hands on her hips. I'd never seen her so mad.

"Double great," I said.

We marched solemnly toward our doom. The closer we got, the more it felt like wading through a vat of peanut butter. No way we'd get off without punishment, and the worst part was that Jason wouldn't even look at me. I was alone.

The yelling started half a block away.

"Annie Lynn Jenkins! Where have you and Jason been this past hour and a half? We've been combing the neighborhood, searching for you two. We've been worried sick."

Mr. Parker didn't say anything, but he didn't have to. The vein on his forehead said it all. Something flickered in his eyes when he saw Jason. Could it have been relief? I doubted. Anger most likely.

My lips trembled against my will.

Jason was furious at me, this trip had been a waste, and now we were probably going to get grounded from each other again. And it was all my fault. Jason hadn't even wanted to go.

"Sorry," I muttered. "About everything."

Jason still wouldn't talk to me. He didn't even glance my direction as he marched toward his dad.

I ran to catch up. He may hate me, but the least I could do was protect him. "Wait! Please. It's my fault." The other adults were already headed back to their houses. "I was so excited to be with Jason, I lost track of time. Don't be mad at him." Jason's mom and dad stood together. I focused on his mom, betting she'd have more mercy. "Jason wanted to come home sooner, but I wouldn't listen, and he didn't want to leave me alone." I dared a glance at my own mom, who shook her head.

"Next time, tell us where you're going so we don't worry," she said. Dad slipped next to her and put his arm around her.

Mr. Parker hadn't taken his eyes from Jason. When he finally looked at me, I thought I'd turn to stone, his gaze was so hard. "I guess two weeks wasn't enough. Let's go, Jason."

I stumbled backward, holding my bike for balance. My vision blurred with tears. I shook my head, struggling to speak. "Please, don't do this." I looked to my mom, silently begging her to fix this. She could fix anything.

But my mom's shoulders slumped.

It was Dad who stepped up. "Ted." He laid a hand on Mr. Parker's shoulder. "Bianca. You remember what it was like as a kid. Surely you missed curfew once or twice."

For a second, Mr. Parker looked like he might cave, but then he shook his head. He put an arm around his wife. "It's not the same world, Sam. They have to learn they can't just disappear like that. If grounding them from each other is what it takes, so be it."

"Ted, please. We know Annie can be . . . impulsive, but she means well. She's a good kid." He smiled at me. "She'll be devastated when you move. They both will."

I looked at Jason, wondering if that was still true.

"Don't take away their last few weeks together. Surely we can find another punishment."

Mr. Parker hesitated. I jumped in.

"Please! I'll do anything. Just don't ground us from each other." I held my breath, afraid that if I moved I'd bump his decision the wrong direction.

Mr. Parker gave a curt nod. "Turkey pen needs cleaning. You two will make it shine like the Taj Mahal. Friday after school."

"The turkey pen?" My mouth went dry.

I snuck a glance at Jason. He was watching me. I blushed because I could read his thoughts. He didn't think I'd do it.

I opened my mouth to prove otherwise, but visions of turkeys filled my head. Gobbling, and feathers, and sharp beaks pecking at me. I closed my mouth.

Jason snorted. "It was nice knowing you, Annie." He pushed his bike toward his home.

And then I remembered. The turkeys would be gone by then. "No, wait! I'll do it."

Jason froze. Then he turned and stared back at me.

I nodded, thoughts racing. This was a sign — it had to be. We were meant to find the treasure. I looked Mr. Parker in the eye and held out my hand. "We'll even bury the turkey droppings for you."

A grin blossomed on Jason's face.

Mr. Parker's reaction wasn't as nice. He stared at my hand but didn't take it. "Fine. But I'm warning you both right now. Any more incidents like this or the nail, and you can say your goodbyes then. You'll be grounded from each other until we move."

20

I adjusted the black pirate cap on my head and pushed up the sleeves of the silky white shirt with the skull-and-crossbone buttons. "Arrgh! Does this be the place, matey?" I pointed to a spot next to the ditch, grinning at Mrs. Schuster who donned a thick velvet jacket and a hook in place of her hand.

Jason flipped up his eye patch. "Do you think I could wear this to school?"

"Maybe for Halloween." *If you're still here*, I thought, then kicked it away. Of course he would be. I mean, Monday had been ominous — Jason mad at me, then almost getting grounded again — but things had worked out perfectly. It'd be the same with the treasure.

Today we'd mark the spot. Friday, tomorrow, we'd find the treasure. Everything would be fine.

Mrs. Schuster sighed, then dug through the haggard pirate satchel slung over her shoulder. "I can't believe I let you two talk me into this. I must be a bigger fool than I thought. And in pirate clothes no less. What must your parents think?"

Despite her words, she smiled. I was glad we'd asked her to come and amazed she'd agreed to the pirate clothes.

With Mr. Parker's edict, we had one shot to uncover the treasure. We needed all the help we could get, and Mrs. Schuster knew the most about Black Marge. Jason still didn't believe in it. But he would after we found it.

Just that morning I'd begged Mrs. Schuster to show Jason and me the journal. Just show us. I didn't even ask to touch it.

"I can't do that," Mrs. Schuster had said. "The thing's cursed. Only direct descendants of Marge can look without being turned into lawn gnomes."

Even I didn't believe that story. But Mrs. Schuster *did* have a large number of gnomes in her backyard. So when she promised to look at the journal for clues and meet us at my house after school, I'd backed down.

With one hand still in her satchel, Mrs. Schuster shook her head. "I can't do this. I'm sorry, but there's something I need to tell you two."

Jason and I froze, certain we were in trouble. Maybe Mr. Parker had hired Mrs. Schuster to spy on us. That might just solve the mystery in one fell swoop.

"What is it?" I asked. "Is the costume too much for you? You don't really have to wear one if you don't want." I hoped that's what it was.

Mrs. Schuster stared at me, her forehead scrunched into one big wrinkle. "No. It's not that. See I . . . I mean . . . well . . . I don't really know where to start. The one hundred steps, that is. This is all in good fun, right? You won't hate me if we don't find the treasure?"

Jason smacked my arm and gave his know-it-all look.

I'd have smacked him back but I didn't want to push it after the whole blabbing-his-secret thing.

Maybe I should have been worried by what Mrs. Schuster said. But I had a good feeling about this dig. Something big was coming. I could feel it.

"Of course we won't hate you." I gave her a hug while Jason shook his head.

"And you won't forget to visit an old lady when this is all over?"

I laughed. "Never."

With another sigh, she extracted a ball of string and a compass from her satchel. "As best I can reckon from the old maps I found, this was the border of the pear orchard. I suggest we walk the one hundred steps here. Jason, go get that boulder for us. That big one right there."

It was so heavy I had to help carry it.

"Now Annie, tie some string around it." She threw the string at me. "This is how we'll make sure we walk in a straight line."

When the string was tied, Mrs. Schuster flipped open the compass. "Either one of you know how to use this thing?"

The spindle bobbed this way and that, finally settling on a direction. "It points north. I think." I'd seen Matt play with his compass, but he'd never let me touch it.

Jason grinned. "I got my orienteering badge last year. I'm pretty good, too."

Mrs. Schuster pressed it into his palm. "Remind me to bequeath this to you before I die. It could use a good home."

"Thank you!" Jason beamed. I could practically see the rays of light shooting from his head. I tried not to feel jealous.

"Now, steer us north, Mr. Navigator. Annie, you hold the string and count."

I wanted to complain. Navigating sounded a lot cooler than holding the string, not to mention getting the compass. But I bit my tongue. I didn't want Mrs. Schuster to think I was a whiner.

Plus, Jason was happy. I didn't want to mess that up. What with the daily whispering and teasing at school, I kept expecting Jason to blow up at me again. But so far he hadn't. I wanted to keep it that way.

I concentrated on stepping evenly. "One . . . two . . ."

At fifty steps out, Mrs. Schuster gasped and clutched her left arm.

"Are you all right?" I dropped the string and put my arm around her. As if I could support her or something.

Her breaths came ragged, her face scrunched with pain. Jason was a Cub Scout. That meant he knew first aid, right? But Jason just stared.

Several seconds passed and Mrs. Schuster stood up straight, breathing heavily. "It's our archenemy, Pirate Blue-Beard and his gang! An arrow skimmed my arm. I thought I was a goner."

Man was I relieved. I almost started laughing. Mrs. Schuster was *good*. I'd really thought she was hurt.

"Arrgh!" I pulled an imaginary sword from my belt and whirled to face the invisible foes. "I can take them! Go on without me. I'll catch up."

Jason jumped in next to me, sword at the ready. "And leave all the fun for you?"

Together we battled our enemies, striking and blocking with style. Nothing and no one stood a chance next to Captain Annie and First Mate Jason.

Mrs. Schuster protected our supplies and pointed out new foes as they arrived. When we'd finally vanquished the enemy, she applauded. "Bravo, me hearties! Excellent work. Black Marge would be proud."

Why couldn't all adults be this fun?

Wiping at my sweaty forehead, I picked up the abandoned ball of string and we counted the steps till we hit the fence. Mrs. Schuster and I waited while Jason ran home to complete the count in his yard.

I noticed Mrs. Schuster still rubbed her left arm, but she couldn't fool me. Not a second time. In my mind, I imagined our next foes, the pirate ghosts, come to reclaim their treasure. I was just about to invent a weapon to kill ghosts when a turkey pecked at the fence. I hopped back, suddenly feeling sick. They were supposed to be gone. Jason had said his dad was selling them this week.

I squeezed my hands into fists to stop them from shaking. *They'll be gone by tomorrow*, I told myself.

But what if they weren't?

Thank heavens for Mrs. Schuster's fidgeting. It gave me something else to think about.

She took several steps toward her house, then shuffled back and peered over the fence. "That boy is sure taking his time." She wrung her hands and headed for the ditch. "You know it's just a guess, right?"

"We *know*," I said. "You've reminded us a bajillion times. We promise not to blame you if it's not there." I almost offered to PB&J-shake on it before I remembered she didn't know about the Society. It just seemed like she should be a member.

"Okay," Mrs. Schuster rubbed her nose. "I just don't think I could bear it if you two were mad at me."

It was weird. For a second she looked like a regular old grandma, all stooped and trembling. She reminded me of my grandpa just before he died. I offered my hand and she took it. "We could never be mad at you." I held on till the trembling slowed.

Mrs. Schuster nodded. She looked like she was going to cry. Adults weren't supposed to do that. I looked away, until Jason called out from his yard.

I ran to the fence and pushed the string through. Jason walked the last five steps, then Mrs. Schuster gave her approval. With a funny old mallet, Jason pounded several pebbles into the dirt. I prayed they would stay put.

One more day. Then everything would be back to normal.

21

When Friday finally came, we were as ready as we'd ever be. I even whistled on the way home from the bus. Sure, there was a chance we wouldn't find the treasure, but I had a good feeling about it.

Everything was coming together, and it couldn't all be coincidence. Yes sir, we were meant to find this treasure. Then Jason could stay and his dad would be nice again. Life would be back to normal, and I wouldn't have to . . .

"We shouldn't dig for the treasure," Jason blurted.

I stopped in my tracks. "We can't quit now. We're this close." I pinched my fingers together.

Jason shuffled his feet and squinted at me. "The thing is, it's been a good week. Dressing up like pirates. Fighting off enemies. Just like we used to. And my dad's been more like himself, too. He even played board games with Mom and me last night. He smiled. He *laughed*, Annie. I can't remember the last time he did that. The treasure hunt's been fun, but we both know it's not real. It's time to stop. Leave well enough alone."

I frowned. "It is real. And what do you mean by 'well enough'? If we don't find the treasure, you have to move. That's not 'well enough' to me."

"Annie, you heard her yesterday. Even Mrs. Schuster doesn't think we'll find the treasure. She looked guiltier than you did when your mom caught you trying to sell your kidney."

"That didn't mean anything! She just doesn't want us to be disappointed. That's all."

Jason's shoulders slumped. Without a word, he hefted his backpack higher and marched toward his house.

A horrible thought struck. I chased after him. "Do you . . . *want* to move?"

Jason turned on me. "Of course I don't! But even if by some miracle the treasure does exist, Mrs. Schuster has no clue where it's buried. So we'll dig a hole, find nothing, and then be grounded for life. It's not worth it."

I relaxed. Jason always worried too much about getting in trouble. I could deal with *that*. "Your dad *said* we could dig a hole. Remember? If there's no treasure, we'll fill the hole back up. With manure, like we promised. How can we possibly get in trouble for that? We have to try. No regrets, right? It'll work out. I have a good feeling about it."

"That's what has me worried," Jason mumbled.

At his house, Jason's mom ushered us into the front room, where Jason's dad sat reading the newspaper. I had to admire her. Despite all their problems, Mrs. Parker still looked amazing. Today she wore a creamy silk button-up with a sleek gray pencil skirt. No jewelry, but it didn't matter.

It struck me that I hadn't seen her dressed up for a while. She'd been in jeans on Monday, but I'd been too afraid of getting grounded from Jason to notice.

She waved us in. "I'll be in the bedroom if you need me, dear."

"Okay, Mom." Jason gave her a kiss on the cheek.

Mr. Parker didn't even look up. "Tools are in the garage. Don't break anything."

"Come on." Jason headed to the back door. "I'll get the rakes . . . *and* shovels. Meet me on the porch." He cut through the kitchen to the garage.

Though we had a disgusting job to do, I shivered with excitement. If we found the treasure, everything would be different. Better.

I skipped outside and nearly puked then and there.

Turkeys.

Strutting in the pen.

Pecking at the ground.

Gobbling like they had a right to be there.

They were supposed to be gone.

I stood frozen in place. I didn't even notice Jason until he shoved a rake at me.

"You okay?"

I glared at him. "You said the turkeys would be gone!"

Jason stepped back. "I did not. We never even talked about turkeys!"

"Last Saturday? On my back porch, eating popsicles? You said your dad was selling them this week."

"He is. *Tomorrow*. That's why he wants us to clean the pen. So he can get a good price. I — I thought you knew." His eyes flicked to the back door. "I thought you agreed to do it anyway. For me."

I swallowed. "I did. But I . . ."

His shoulders slumped. "I see."

I gripped the deck railing and stared at the wretched, strutting beasts. I'd promised Mr. Parker. *Begged* for this punishment. And Society members keep their word. But how to make my legs move toward the turkeys when all I wanted to do was run?

Without another word, Jason laid down the extra rake and shovel. He trudged down the porch steps and headed for the pen. Alone.

My hands trembled. My chest burned, and I struggled to breathe.

I thought of Black Marge facing down Leonard the Lout. Jason riding to the bank when he didn't want to. The look on Jason's face when I said I'd clean the turkey pen to save our friendship.

"Jason, wait!" Before I could change my mind, I grabbed the tools and ran to catch up. "I'm sorry. I said I'd do it, and I will."

His mouth dropped open. "Really?"

I nodded.

We tramped to the turkey pen and Jason unlatched the gate. He paused. "Hey! I could lock them in their house. Would that help?"

I took in the rickety old shed they called a turkey house. It looked like it might fall down any time. But it was better than nothing. "That'd be great."

He slipped into the pen and herded the beasts using his fan-shaped rake. When the last one was in the house, he slammed the door and locked it from the outside.

Sweat trickled down my back, though the weather was cool. *I can do this*, I told myself. *I can do this*. I felt like the little engine that could.

I pushed open the gate and shuddered at the little white and green piles all over the ground. They were mushed in turkey claw prints, or smeared in the shape of a shoe. I took a deep breath, plugged my nose, and walked in.

Jason had already started raking. "I'll work here by the turkey house and manure pile. You can start by the tree." He pointed to the far side of the pen. "There are fewer droppings over there."

I nodded and was about to say "thanks" when I noticed the big green pile of sludge behind Jason. "Is that all poop?"

Jason laughed. "It's called manure. Grass clippings mixed with poop."

"Oh." Just the sight of it made my eyes water, not to mention the burning stench that suddenly struck. Doggie doo-doo times ten. I wished I'd brought a nose plug.

Grateful I'd be as far from it all as possible, I tip-toed around the piles and began work in my assigned quadrant.

It went quickly, but the indignity of it grated on my nerves with each stroke. Cap'n Black Marge would never be reduced to the poop galley. I imagined myself as the captain and grinned wickedly as I passed the job on to Mr. Parker.

"Arrgh! You can scrub the poop deck or walk the plank," Cap'n Annie said.

First Mate Jason passed his dad a mop. "And no lollygaggin', yeh scallywag, or you can forget about yer ration of protein paste!"

I was so involved with my daydream, I never saw it coming.

Gobble, gobble!

A flurry of feathers landed on my shoulder. I screamed as claws dug into my skin. I slapped at the bird to get it off, but the beast clung tighter, squawking and flapping with more energy. Feathered wings smacked me in the face. A beak pecked at my ear.

"Get it off! Get it off!" Blinded by the mass of wild bird in my face, I chose a direction and ran. When Jason started yelling, I followed the sound.

"No! Annie, stop!"

I deciphered his words just before slamming into him. The turkey finally let go at impact, but with the momentum, it flew smack into the wall of the turkey house. Jason and I splatted into the manure pile.

We sat there, stunned, until Jason slapped his hand in the muck. "Why don't you listen? I told you to stop! You were scaring that bird senseless with all your screaming and flapping."

My jaw dropped. My shoulder stung where the turkey had clawed me, my shirt was ripped, and my pride had taken a mortal blow. But the injustice of Jason's words burned the worst. I wiped green slime from my face before grabbing a handful and chucking it at him. The manure bomb exploded on his chest. "That bird came from nowhere! You were supposed to lock them up!"

"If you weren't such a chicken, it wouldn't have mattered." A green blob sailed past my ear.

I got him on the arm as one exploded on my leg. I slogged to my knees to better attack when the door of the turkey house slammed open.

A gobbling mass of feathers and beaks tumbled from the structure and headed straight for the gate. The one I'd forgotten to close. I froze in terror.

Jason sprinted to stop the flock. It was too late.

Turkeys poured into the yard and squawked their way to the garden. I hadn't known the creatures could hack through a zucchini plant so easily.

"Annie, help!" Jason glanced anxiously at the back door. "Shoo! Go on!" Waving his rake at the birds, he attempted to herd them back to the pen. "Annie, please!" The strain in his voice was like a slap to the face.

My life flashed before my eyes — cowering in fear while Jason chased away the turkey on the kindergarten field trip; facing down a bully in first grade with a quaking

Jason at my side; burying my Miss Piggy alarm clock while Jason stood guard; pleading with the man at the bank; and confronting Jason's dad. There was hardly a memory without Jason in it. He had been there for everything. Even the rotten stuff. Even when he was scared.

The truth of the situation struck hard. This was it. When Jason's dad saw this mess, our friendship was over. And how was I going to end it? By hiding while he struggled alone? I couldn't do that. Jason certainly wouldn't.

I imagined I was back on Black Marge's ship. Blue Beard's pirates streamed onto our boat, cutlasses glinting in the sun. Only I, Cap'n Annie, could save them.

Grabbing my rake — er, sword — I charged the battle. "I'm coming, Jas—" something caught my foot just outside the gate, and I belly-flopped to the ground. I threw a dirty look at the offending object, but when I saw what it was, I caught my breath.

The garden hose.

I left my rake where it lay, grabbed the hose and dashed to the spigot. With the water on high, I sent a quick spurt at Jason with my thumb.

"Hey!" He swung around, ready to fight.

I held up the hose. "I'll spray, you herd."

Jason grinned. "Great idea."

I hoped the turkeys wouldn't attack me for spraying them. Thumb over the water, I aimed at a fat one feasting on a tomato bush.

Gobbles broke out on contact. The bird tumbled backward and immediately retreated. I inched forward thinking only of my aim.

The turkey tried to get back to the garden, but I sprayed it again. The bird ran toward Jason, who stood waiting in a football stance. Another shot, and Jason herded it into the pen.

One by one, we cornered the turkeys until they were all back inside. Jason thunked the gate latch down, then joined me by the spigot.

After spraying the mud, manure, and feathers off ourselves as best we could, we surveyed the damage. The grass was flooded. It looked more like a rice paddy than a yard. Except, of course, for the feathers floating on top. *The water will go away*, I told myself. *The grass will look fine once it's mowed*. Surely Jason's dad wouldn't banish me for this.

But one glance at the garden and my hope died. It barely resembled a garden anymore. Several cornstalks hung limp, snapped in two by the weight of the turkeys. The rows of zucchini, squash, and lettuce looked like a mesh of leaves and mud with mushed and half-pecked vegetables sticking out at odd spots. *Garden soup*, I thought.

Jason barely moved. He stared at the garden, horror on his face.

My chest tightened. It hurt to breathe. "Maybe if we . . ."

"Annie." Jason held up a hand.

Then someone gasped.

Jason's mom stood on the porch. Her hand fluttered in front of her open mouth as she gazed at the garden. The next instant, Mr. Parker boomed out the back door. "What the . . ." His shocked gaze swept over the mess, then turned on us.

The turkeys gobbled in the background as though telling their side of the story. I tensed for a lecture.

It never came.

Mr. Parker pulled his wife into a hug and she buried her face in his chest. After a moment, he whispered into her ear and kissed her forehead. Step by slow step, he moved to the garden. With a gentleness I hadn't seen in him for a long time, he brushed his hand over a broken cornstalk. He picked up a smashed tomato then let it drop.

When he turned to face his wife, I was shocked to see tears in his eyes. He shook his head.

Mrs. Parker's hand tightened over her mouth. Tears poured down her cheeks.

I didn't get it. If he was so mad, why didn't he just yell at us? But tears? Why would . . .

And then it struck. Vegetable Yuck. Jason's switch to school lunches. His huge appetite at Mrs. Schuster's breakfasts.

They were living off the garden.

Jason had never said anything, but one peek at him told me it was true. He stood hunched in the pen, staring at the ground. I felt smaller than a turkey dropping.

When the sound of the phone jangled through the back door, Mrs. Parker stumbled inside, then called in her husband.

I slowly turned. "Jason, I . . ."

He shook his head; there was a look in his eyes I'd never seen before. "Don't. Annie, just go."

"But I can't . . ."

"For once in your life just listen to me! I want to be alone." He turned his back on me and raked at the turkey droppings with force.

I wiped at my drippy nose, struggling not to cry. Ever so gently I leaned the rake against the house, then with a sob, sloshed across the yard and exited out the fence gate. I didn't stop running until I was under my bed.

That's when I remembered the treasure.

I could kick myself. I'd been so caught up in saving his house, I hadn't even asked how Jason was doing. My best friend barely had enough to eat, and I hadn't noticed. How could I be so selfish? How could I even call myself a friend?

I wished I'd never gotten that stupid treasure map. Now I was glad it had burned. But it wasn't enough. I stumbled to my dresser and pulled out the list. With a jerk I tore it in half, then again and again till it was too small to rip.

22

"Ow!" I cringed as my mom yanked a brush through my hair. In normal circumstances, I'd never let my mom touch it, but the dried-on manure was a nightmare. Even after washing it a few times.

"Almost done." Mom grabbed some hair and pulled.

"That hurts!" I jerked away.

"Do you want me to cut it off?" The expression on her face said she just might do it.

I grudgingly sat back up.

"Now hold still."

I gritted my teeth while my mom stuck a thousand needles in my head. At least that's what it felt like. It took all I had not to complain.

"There, I think that's the last tangle. Let's try not to fall into any more manure piles, okay? Or at least wash your hair a little sooner next time." She sat on the bed next to me, her flower-print scrubs soft from so many washings.

I snuggled in, enjoying the fresh smell of detergent and cucumber body wash. All the smells that said "home." All the smells that seemed gone from my life lately.

"Did you talk to them yet?" I wanted to ask if Jason and I were grounded from each other, but I kind of didn't want to know. Besides, how could I worry about that when Jason's family was starving? I stared at my feet, pretending they were fascinating.

Mom gave me a squeeze. "They're still not answering, sweet pea. But you can't blame yourself for the garden. That bird attacked you. It's not your fault."

"*I* left the gate open."

"And they chose to keep turkeys. Sometimes these things just happen. Your dad left a bag of food on their porch, plus he saw Mr. Parker slaughter a turkey. They won't starve in one night."

I sniffed. Sure they'd be fine for a night or two, but what about all the other nights after that?

Mom glanced at her watch and sighed. "It's nearly nine. I've got to go. Kate's at a friend's tonight, but if you need anything or your shoulder starts to hurt, your dad's watching a movie with Matt downstairs. Okay?"

"Okay." I sat on my bed and listened to the creak of the stairs. Mom's voice floated up as she said goodbye to Matt and Dad.

When the hum of the automatic garage door started, I flipped off the lights and ran to the window. I wanted to cram in every last second with my mom. So what if she was driving away? Maybe if I willed it hard enough, she'd turn around and come home.

The car turned the corner. I kept watch, hoping for that miracle. Hoping the car would suddenly come back. It didn't.

I stared at the empty street for a long time before noticing Mrs. Schuster's house. The lights were on and the garage was open. I glanced at the alarm clock though I knew the time. Mrs. Schuster was usually in bed by now. Should I check on her?

Something clinked against the window and I jumped. I peered down at the yard. My heart *ka-thumped*. Jason was there. He motioned for me to come out.

I bolted for the door. Did he have news of the punishment? Maybe the garden wasn't as bad as we'd thought. I crossed my fingers.

Outside, Jason waited by the corner of the house. A duffle bag sat next to him. "I'm running away," he said. "I came to say goodbye."

"What?" I shivered in my soccer pajamas. "Why?"

Jason shifted from foot to foot. "You can't talk me out of it. It's my fault about the garden. I saw the open gate and didn't do anything."

"*I'm* the one who left it open."

"I should've fastened the turkey house door better."

"That stupid turkey knocked it open. You couldn't help that."

"And I should have counted the birds when I locked them up. There were only ten. It wouldn't have been that hard. Then none of this would have happened."

"Only ten? I thought you had way more than that."

He shrugged. "Let's just say I'd be fine if I never ate another bite of turkey the rest of my life."

"Oh." I stared at the ground. I should have realized. "Jason, you can't . . ."

"I'm leaving," he said. "You can't talk me out of it. It'll be one less mouth to feed. One less worry for my parents."

I recognized that expression on his face. It didn't happen very often, but he could be more stubborn than me. I wanted to cry. One more thing to add to my list of reasons to feel guilty. I'd read *The Thief Lord* and seen *Oliver Twist*. I knew what happened to runaways. First stealing, then jail. And of course, I'd have to brave some daring rescue to free him. It would be an adventure, but Jason would never last in jail. I knew.

There was only one solution. "I'm coming with you."

Jason started to smile then frowned. "You can't. I won't let you."

"Since when has that stopped me?"

Jason crossed his arms. "You're not coming. You're in your pajamas and you don't have your stuff. I'll just leave when you're inside."

I resented the smug grin on his face. Two could play at that game. I shifted to interrogation mode. "Did you pack enough food?"

The smug look fell away. "I'm not taking any of their food. I'm a Cub Scout. I'll make do."

"Cub Scouts." I rolled my eyes. "Do you have a fishing pole?"

"No."

"A knife?"

"No, but . . ."

"Any money?"

"Thirty-two dollars." He lifted his chin.

"Where will you go?"

"I can't tell you."

"Uh-huh. Let me guess, you plan to take the bus."

"Annie, I'll be fine!" Jason grabbed his bag and started walking away. "I just came to say goodbye. So goodbye!"

I ran after him. "At least let me make you some sandwiches."

Jason didn't stop. "And why don't we announce to the world that I'm running away while we're at it?"

"Mom's gone and Dad's watching a movie. No one will see you."

Jason spun around. "I can't risk it. Plus, I don't want to put you in danger. They'll ask you first, you know. That's why I won't tell you where I'm going." For the first time that night, Jason smiled. "I've got it all figured out."

If I wasn't so worried, I might have laughed. "All except the food, you mean. I'm not letting you go without food."

"And I'm not going inside your house." Jason picked up his duffle bag,

I glanced across the cul-de-sac at Mrs. Schuster's still-lit house. Maybe she could talk some sense into Jason. "What if we ask Mrs. Schuster? She'll help."

Jason shook his head again. "She's a grown-up. They have to report runaways. It's like a rule or something. I'll be fine."

"We could leave your bag outside. We don't have to say *why* we want the food."

"She's old, not stupid. It's nine o'clock at night. Where would we be going?"

"We'll tell her it's for the treasure hunt. That we want to go early tomorrow morning and don't want to disturb our parents."

Jason snorted. "I'm leaving."

I stepped in front of him. "You're right. That was dumb. But what about the compass? She was going to give it to you, and it would help you get where you're going."

Jason's face softened. I could see in his eyes how much he wanted it.

"We'll knock and tell her we saw her garage door open, that we wanted to check on her. Then we can ask about the compass, and you know Mrs. Schuster — she's sure to offer us food."

Jason stared at the house a long time. "You promise not to say anything?"

I slugged him in the arm. Hard. "That's for calling me a tattletale."

Jason scowled at me and rubbed his arm. "Well what are you going to say when she asks why we're out so late?"

"We'll tell her we snuck out to say goodbye after the turkey incident."

Jason left his bag in the shadow of a tree and we walked to the door. Normally I would just go in, but being so late, I didn't think that was a good idea. The green-goo-faced, open-housecoat version of Mrs. Schuster still haunted my dreams.

A minute passed. I glanced at Jason and knocked again. I was starting to get worried. "Her car's in the garage, right?"

Jason peeked. "Yep."

She had to be home. I tried the knob. Unlocked. The door creaked open.

"Hello?"

Nothing. I bit my lip as we stepped into the house. "Mrs. Schuster?"

Still no answer.

We crept to the kitchen. "Mrs. Schuster?"

The dirty dinner dishes were still in the sink. Mrs. Schuster was the cleanest person I knew. My heart beat like a drum in a parade. It was so loud, I bet Jason could hear it.

"Mrs. Schuster!" I was frantic. I ran into the dining room and stopped dead. She lay facedown on the ground, paper scattered around her. A half-eaten piece of pie was still on the table.

I dropped to my knees ready to shake her, then stopped. Hadn't my mom said not to move someone who's unconscious? Instead I lifted her wrist — that's what they always did in the movies. I couldn't feel anything. Panic rose in my throat. Vomit flavored. My mom had talked about this. I should have known what to do, but I couldn't focus. I could barely breathe.

"Is she breathing?" Jason stood behind me.

I shook my head. "I don't know."

Jason pulled on my shoulder. "Call nine-one-one. I'll get your dad."

I numbly obeyed as Jason sprinted out the door. My hands were shaking when I dialed.

"Nine-one-one. What is your emergency?"

I stuttered out the story, trying not to cry.

"An ambulance is on the way, darling. Can you take the phone outside to watch for them?"

When I got to the door my dad was already running across Mrs. Schuster's lawn. I passed the phone to him and hurried back inside. Jason followed.

I gripped Mrs. Schuster's hand and she stirred. Her eyes fluttered.

Relief felt like a warm blanket. "Mrs. Schuster! Can you hear me?"

"Is that . . . Annie?" Her raspy voice whispered.

"Yes, yes. And Jason's here, too. We've called nine-one-one. Everything will be fine. Just hang in there." I'd never understood how you could cry for joy, but now it made sense. It was all I could do to keep from sobbing in gratitude.

Sirens started in the distance, getting closer and louder, blocking out Mrs. Schuster's labored breathing. She beckoned me closer. "Getting old . . . stinks." She slogged back into unconsciousness as the room exploded in a flurry of activity.

Jason and I backed away when two paramedics rolled an equipment-filled gurney into the room. One thumped two red bags to the floor. The other slid a long board onto the floor next to Mrs. Schuster. The scene felt unreal, like being caught inside a TV show.

My dad scooted next to me and put his arm around me. Dazed, I watched the men work, hardly registering the questions they asked. At one point Dad left and came back holding several prescription bottles.

I held my breath when the men strapped an oxygen mask over Mrs. Schuster's mouth and nose. I clung to my dad when they slid the board under her. I wanted to cry when they covered her with blankets and strapped her in place. It couldn't be Mrs. Schuster lying there.

Two more men came in and before I knew it, they were rolling her out.

I didn't move. I couldn't watch the ambulance doors close on her. I couldn't.

Dad gave a sympathetic nod, then followed them out.

"I'm sorry." Jason broke the silence.

I wouldn't look at him. Instead, I jumped to my feet, suddenly afraid of the stillness. "We should clean up." I scooped up the scattered papers intending to lay them on the table, but the signature at the bottom caught my eye. *Marge Schuster.* The writing was clear. "She never told us she was named after Black Marge." It was good to concentrate on something other than what had just happened.

"Seriously?" Jason scooted closer and I held the papers so he could see.

That's when I realized. These were the papers. THE papers. The ones that could solve the mystery.

I knew I shouldn't read the letter, but my eyes were already skimming. It was dated almost five years ago.

Dear Mr. Philmore,

As per our conversation, I've included with this letter a copy of my daughter's birth certificate. There you will also find my full name as well as that of the father, Leonard C. Hawkins . . .

Leonard? I frowned. Mrs. Schuster's husband was named Ned, I was sure of it. And she only had a son — the picture evidence was on the wall before us. A glance at Jason told me he'd read it too. We stared at each other in confusion.

"Annie? Jason?"

I whipped around at my dad's voice, hiding the letter behind me.

"Are you ready?" Dad rubbed his eyes, then straightened his glasses. His shoulders were hunched and he looked like he had just weeded the entire garden on his own.

With a sniff, I nodded. "Just let me wash these dishes. Mrs. Schuster wouldn't leave a mess." I slipped the papers under the plate, then stacked silverware and a cup on top.

In the kitchen, I set the dishes in the sink, then folded the letters as small as I could. I wrapped them in my fist, hoping Dad wouldn't notice. Curses on pajamas with no pockets.

23

I waited at the curb while my dad walked Jason to the door. I wrapped my arms around myself and shivered in the night air. At least it was easier to hide the letter that way.

A minute passed before the porch light flipped on. Jason's dad opened the door, and his mouth settled into a frown. I hoped there wouldn't be a scene.

My dad spoke first and I watched his gestures, wishing I could hear the words. Jason stared at the ground. Mr. Parker crossed his arms like he was a drill sergeant or something. Finally, my dad handed over the duffle bag, and Mr. Parker stepped aside to let Jason in.

When the door clicked shut, my stomach flip-flopped. Was Jason in big trouble? Did Mr. Parker blame me? And most importantly, were we grounded from each other? I guessed "yes" on all three.

My dad put his arm around me. "You did good tonight, sweet pea."

And the next thing I knew, I was crying. I buried my face in his shirt, smelling sweat mingled with the fading spice of his aftershave. "Will they be okay?"

"The Parkers? I think so."

"But I ruined their garden." My lips trembled. I hated that, but it was my fault. "What are they going to eat?"

I was surprised when my dad laughed. "You have such a big heart. I love that about you." He adjusted his glasses. "Do you really think we'd let them starve?"

The pit in my stomach eased a little. I let my dad's warmth and steadiness wrap me up. It was nice having him around, I decided.

We turned the corner and there stood Mrs. Schuster's now-dark house. I gripped the letter tighter in my hand. An image of Mrs. Schuster crumpled on the floor flashed through my mind. I heard the sirens, felt her papery hand in mine. The question I'd avoided couldn't wait.

"Will Mrs. Schuster die?"

The smile on Dad's face faded. He wouldn't look at me. "I hope not, sweet pea. I hope not."

***

I lay awake wondering if I was cursed. First Jason, and now Mrs. Schuster. How could I lose two friends in one day? Had I broken an unspoken Society protocol when I'd tried to bury those sandwiches without Jason? Or maybe I shouldn't have suggested a mass burial instead of thirteen separate ones. Or maybe it had nothing to do with the Society. Maybe Black Marge's treasure really was cursed.

When I was sure Dad had fallen asleep, I flipped on the light. Thank heavens Kate was at a friend's.

Sitting cross-legged on my bed, I unfolded the papers that I'd hidden under my pillow. I knew they were important, but now they seemed dire. Mrs. Schuster had been reading them when she fell.

They were well worn and if I hadn't noticed them before, I could have guessed she looked at them a lot. Mrs. Schuster clearly had a secret, and I was going to figure it out. Maybe it would even help her get better.

I re-read the first page.

Dear Mr. Philmore,

As per our conversation, I have included with this letter a copy of my daughter's birth certificate. There you will also find my full name as well as that of the father, Leonard C. Hawkins. I left the abusive lout before she was born, and I gave her up for adoption at birth because I had no means to care for her. I was eighteen at the time. As I stated before, I do not wish to intrude on my daughter. I just want a chance to explain. To tell her how much I loved her, and still love her . . . even if it isn't returned.

I stared at the page in shock. Mrs. Schuster *did* have a secret past. A tragic past! Suddenly my cheeks felt hot. Guilt struck like a flyswatter. I shouldn't be reading these papers. Solving a mystery was one thing, but prying into someone's personal life was something else. Besides, I didn't see how this could explain Mrs. Schuster's sudden interest in me and Jason.

I was dying to know how the story ended. I wanted to keep reading. Like, a lot. But it wasn't worth the guilt. I started to fold the letters back up when the letterhead caught my eye: *Edward & Margaret Schuster.*

Something clicked in my brain.

Edward. The name of Black Marge's husband. I scanned down to the name of the ex-husband. Leonard. Lenny the lout.

Mrs. Schuster's voice echoed in my mind: *Lenny really wasn't a lout in the beginning, you know . . . I mean, according to Black Marge.*

I hadn't questioned it at the time, but now I saw it for what it was. Mrs. Schuster had been telling her *own* story. She'd corrected herself to sell it as Black Marge's.

And hadn't she used the last name "Smith"? Edward Smith. Only the most common last name ever. Then there was the journal I could never see. And protein paste? Right. How convenient to have a story about peanut butter when she was fixing my peanut butter and jelly sandwich. The clues had been there all along.

Anger built up in my chest as I thought of all the lies Mrs. Schuster had told us. She'd not only let two kids hunt for a non-existent treasure, but she'd strung us along on a wild goose chase.

In my mind, I saw Mrs. Schuster being rolled out of the room on a gurney. My anger fizzled. I couldn't be mad at her when she was lying in a hospital on the brink of death. But I wanted answers. I wanted to know why Mrs. Schuster had lied. It just didn't make sense.

With only a little hesitation, I turned the page. It was a short note from the Philmore guy.

. . . Nothing to report at this time. . . .

I flipped the page.

. . . Nothing to report. . . .

Again.

. . . Nothing at this time. . . .

The dates were spread out over years, and I could almost feel the frustration of the long process. I guessed Mrs. Schuster hadn't found the daughter yet, or she wouldn't still be reading these letters. I wished I could comfort her. Encourage her to keep going. Keep searching. Hopefully I'd get the chance.

The second-to-last letter was dated just last August, the most recent I'd seen.

Dear Mrs. Schuster,

I regret to inform you that your daughter, Mrs. Elizabeth Mason, has refused contact with you. Please see her enclosed letter for full details. As this report will close this account, I have also enclosed the final bill for my services. Should you have any questions, feel free to contact me . . .

I couldn't move. My heart felt like lead. No! This wasn't how it was supposed to end. After all that searching, how could the daughter just refuse to see her without giving her a chance? It was so unfair. Isn't that what Mrs. Schuster had said? *Life isn't always fair. Just ask Marge.*

I wanted to smack Mrs. Elizabeth Mason. Tell her what she was missing out on. Tell her how awesome Mrs. Schuster would be as a mom.

The last page was the letter from the daughter.

Dear Mr. Philmore,

Please inform your client that I have no interest in meeting or receiving any letters from her. You may let her know that I have a ten-year-old daughter, but in exchange, I ask that she not try to contact us again.

Sincerely,

Mrs. Elizabeth Mason

My hands trembled. The age of Mrs. Mason's daughter trumpeted from the page. The same age as me. Now it all made sense. It could be no coincidence that Mrs. Schuster had given me that treasure chest just weeks after receiving this letter. I wanted to resent it, but too many good memories got in the way.

I wasn't sure how long I sat there before tucking the letters into a drawer and turning off the light. Even then, I couldn't sleep. I stared into the darkness worrying about my friends. I felt helpless. Powerless to change anything.

Just look at how things had turned out with Jason. How could I have thought that *I* could save his house? The idea was laughable. I couldn't even get him to accept sandwiches from me when facing starvation.

I rolled onto my side, trying to get comfortable. Why did this have to happen to the Parkers? Why were they losing their house when so many others had more than enough? I thought of Lila with her designer wardrobe, Prada bag, *and* iPhone. Life was so unfair.

Why couldn't we have ruined the Pierces' garden, instead? I wondered. *They could afford it.*

And then the idea struck, like a dollop of peanut butter on fresh bread. I grinned. I had a plan.

24

I woke up to the smell of grilled cheese. I breathed it in, enjoying the scent until I realized what it meant: lunch. My eyes flew open and I ripped the covers off. The sun streamed in through the windows and the alarm clock read 12:32.

"Aw man!" I smacked my forehead. If I wanted to pull off my plan, I didn't have a second to waste. Not to mention that I'd missed soccer. I hurried and changed, then ran to the kitchen.

Dad, Kate, and Matt sat around the table.

"Morning, sleepyhead. I thought you earned a little extra sleep after last night." Dad pointed to a plate of blackened sandwiches. "You're just in time for lunch."

"Hey, cheesebreath." Matt spoke through bites of sandwich. "You owe us. We had to do all the chores."

"Chew with your mouth closed!" Kate stuck her nose in the air. "But the cretin's right. You owe us big time."

I plopped into a chair next to Dad and stuck my tongue out at Matt and Kate.

"Let's be nice." Dad pointed a finger at each of us, but his eyes twinkled. "We can't have your mother thinking I let you go wild."

I dug through the pile to find the least-burned sandwich. Though I was hungry, I couldn't eat till I'd explained my plan. It was urgent. "So I have this idea."

Kate rolled her eyes.

"We're not the only ones with a garden. What if all the neighbors gave food to the Parkers and left it on their doorstep in secret? That way they can't refuse it!"

I waited for all their bad vibes — especially Kate's — but no one said anything. All three of them stared with funny expressions on their faces.

"What?" I sat up straight. "I thought it was a good idea."

Dad finally smiled. "It's a brilliant idea, Annie. I only wish I'd thought of it myself."

Kate sniffed. "I can talk to Emma's parents. Her dad works for a bread company and gets day-old bread for free all the time."

"I can get my friends to do sneaky drop-offs throughout the day." Matt rubbed his hands together. "Ding-dong ditch is our specialty."

"You guys will really help? On a Saturday?" I was stunned.

Kate shrugged. "For once you have a good idea. Just don't let it go to your head."

Matt grinned. "Are you kidding? The chance to ding-dong ditch without getting in trouble? Invaluable practice! . . . Uh, I mean to do future good deeds, of course." He threw a wide-eyed look at Dad, who frowned.

With everyone's approval, I thought I'd burst with excitement. Finally, I could really help. This felt better than searching for some non-existent treasure. It even felt better than solving a real-life mystery.

"I'll sneak into our room for the neighborhood phone list," Dad said when we'd finished eating. "We can make the calls downstairs, where we won't disturb your mother. I'm really proud of you, Annie."

List in hand, I started with the Pierces since they'd given me the idea. I just hoped Lila didn't answer. She hadn't spoken to me since she apologized about Jessica and Jenny. If she answered, she'd probably just hang up.

"Hello?" Mrs. Pierce answered after the first ring.

"Hi. This is Annie Jenkins."

"Annie! We missed you at the soccer game today."

"Yeah, um . . ."

"We heard about what happened though. You are such a brave girl. That must have been really scary."

"Yes, but . . ."

"And poor Mrs. Schuster. We're all just praying she's okay. But look at me, chattering on. I bet you called to talk to Lila. Let me go . . ."

"Wait, Mrs. Pierce!" My head was spinning. Now I knew where Lila got it from. "I called to talk to you."

"Me?" She sounded surprised.

"Yes. The thing is . . ." I hesitated. Lila had probably already blabbed to her parents, but I still didn't want to tell the Parkers' secret to everyone. "The Parkers could use some help." I left it at that and explained my plan about getting all the neighbors to help as simply as I could. "Matt and his friends can pick up your donation and secretly deliver it so the Parkers don't know where it came from."

"Oh honey. Aren't you the sweetest thing? Of course we'd love to be involved. Who else have you called, and what are they bringing?"

"You're the first," I said. "But I was going to call as many people in the neighborhood as I could."

"Have you planned for a base camp to collect the food? Your house is too obvious if you want to keep it secret."

"Base camp?"

"I imagine a lot of people will want to help. You'll need to organize the drop-offs. And your brother can't possibly make it to everyone's house *and* deliver the items. Tell you what. I'll call the Garcias since they have that big new garage. Plus they live just around the corner from the Parkers. I'm sure Judy would be happy to help. You have everyone deliver their offerings there, and Judy and I can organize it for Matt and his friends to deliver."

I was speechless. I hadn't thought beyond getting people to donate. But more than that, I was surprised. I'd always pictured the Pierces as show-offs. Trying to make the rest of us feel bad by reminding us of all the stuff we didn't have. Like Lila always did. I never would have guessed in a million years Mrs. Pierce would offer to help like that. I decided to give her an out. Just in case.

"But . . . are you sure? It might take the whole day."

"Oh Annie, this is much more exciting than my plans at the spa. Even adults like a little adventure now and again. Lila can wait for our little outing. In fact, I bet she'll want to help, too."

The rest of the afternoon raced by with phone calls. My dad and I went alphabetically through the directory and took turns explaining the plan to the neighbors.

The Aarons offered a box of fresh-picked apples. The Braddocks promised bags of vegetables. The Chois had packages of spaghetti from Mr. Choi's work. The Drakes had several bottles of homemade salsa. Even Mrs. O'Reilly, who had very little herself (Dad insisted we call her so she didn't feel left out), offered to stop by the Parkers later in the day with some handyman question so she could innocently offer to help preserve some of the produce.

That's when I realized we'd better spread the donations over the coming weeks. Mrs. Garcia generously offered her husband's garage as our base for as long as we needed, so Dad and I made a schedule and promised to give everyone reminder calls as their donation time got closer. The Parkers would have food for at least the next month — and a better variety than their garden would have given.

When Matt did the first drop-off, I had to resist the urge to stand at the corner and watch. Not that I had time — by four o'clock, we were only to the Ps.

When I hung up the phone with Mrs. Sanchez, who offered carrots and potatoes, the phone rang almost immediately. I let Dad answer.

"Yes, that was my daughter." After a long pause and a series of "uh-huhs," his face erupted in a grin. "Still, that's wonderful news. And I'm sure Annie would be thrilled. . . . Uh-huh . . . yes . . . seven o'clock. We'll see you there. I look forward to meeting you."

When he finally said goodbye, I pounced. "Well?"

"That was Mrs. Schuster's son calling from the hospital. He says his mother is doing very well. 'Back to her cranky self,' he says. He's invited you and Jason to visit tonight. Seven o'clock, before visiting hours are over. She's been insisting on it. Says she threatened to not take her meds if he didn't extend the invitation immediately."

I was relieved Mrs. Schuster was doing so well, and I was excited to go see her. Mostly. Now that I knew the truth, my stomach flip-flopped over what to say to her. Did I confess that I'd read the letters? Did I wait until Mrs. Schuster confessed?

I liked that option best. As long as Mrs. Schuster didn't want to tell another story about Cap'n Black Marge.

25

The sterile smell of the hospital overpowered me when the doors whooshed open. I gripped the bouquet of flowers tighter. Hospitals made me nervous.

In the waiting area, Jason jumped up from his chair with a big grin and ran over. His dad shuffled after him. "I've been dying to talk to you, but your line's been busy."

My face suddenly felt hot. I hadn't thought of that. "Probably Kate. She's always hogging the phone." I couldn't look him in the eye. Even if the lie *was* for his own good.

"It's been amazing, Annie! People have been leaving boxes of food on our porch. Anything you could want: bread, eggs, vegetables, fruit. We've tried to catch them, but it's like magic. The doorbell keeps ringing, the boxes keep appearing, and not a trace of who's doing it! I thought it was you until the fourth or fifth time it happened. I knew there was no way you could have gone so long without getting caught."

"I could have done it!" I bristled at the insult.

"Did you?" Jason asked.

He had me there. "Well . . . no," I grumped.

Jason crossed his arms looking all smug.

"That's what I thought."

It totally stunk that I couldn't argue, but I didn't want to give myself away. Plus, Jason's dad now stood behind him. I clamped my mouth shut, hoping Mr. Parker wouldn't remember that Jason and I were supposed to be grounded from each other. I thought.

It caught me completely off-guard when Jason's dad smiled at me as he shook my dad's hand.

"Bianca is with Mrs. O'Reilly canning the produce we won't be able to eat fast enough. We're simply floored by it all. We wish we knew who to thank —" he eyed me and I batted my eyes all innocent-like — "but whoever is doing it must know us pretty well. I'm not sure I could accept it if I had a place to send it back to."

I didn't dare look at my dad. It was hard enough keeping the grin off my face.

Mr. Parker hesitated, then went all serious. "Frankly, it's a godsend. Last night after you left, Jason prayed for a miracle I knew wouldn't happen. But I was wrong." His voice was husky, and I could practically see the pride for his son beaming from his eyes. "I-It's been humbling. We have good neighbors."

I know an opportunity when I see one. I cleared my throat. "So . . . um . . . does this mean we're not grounded from each other?"

Mr. Parker looked surprised. His cheeks even went a little pink. "You're not grounded. And I'm sor— well, you're always welcome at our house."

I thought my face would crack from grinning — Jason's too. "Thank you!" I was so happy I thought I might float away. It wasn't until my dad nudged me that I remembered we were in a hospital.

"Mrs. Schuster will be waiting. We'd better go."

We rode up the elevator to the fourth floor with Jason giving a play-by-play of the soccer game I missed.

"Lila was playing forward, just standing there admiring her new fake nails, when Bryce cleared the ball. So it sails over everyone and smacks Lila right on her hand, breaking three nails. You would've thought she got mugged! They stopped the game to get her off the field."

A week ago I would have laughed. Somehow, it didn't seem as funny now.

"Here we are. Room four fifteen." Dad knocked on the partially opened door.

A swarm of butterflies filled my gut. *Just act normal*, I told myself. Still, I stayed behind my dad.

Jason nudged me. "The papers?" he mouthed.

I patted the lump in my back pocket wishing I could tell him the story. But that was impossible with our dads right there. "Later," I mouthed back.

"Well don't just stand in the doorway." Mrs. Schuster's voice snapped at us. "You're the first people I've actually *wanted* to see all day."

I followed everyone in. When I saw Mrs. Schuster, I almost had my own heart attack. I wanted to hide my face in my dad's shirt.

Lying in that bed, Mrs. Schuster looked even older than usual, if that was possible. Her grayish hair stuck up at odd angles. Her ashen face matched the white hospital walls, except for the black rings under her eyes.

Machines surrounded the bed, beeping like time bombs ready to go off. Tubes were strung from Mrs. Schuster's hand to mysterious bags of liquid. Another tube lay across her face with prongs up her nose.

Gross.

Dad pulled me forward. "We're glad to see you doing so well. We brought you these." He elbowed me.

I held up the roses, but what I really wanted to do was puke. *Doing so well?* Mrs. Schuster didn't look like she was doing well at all! She looked like she'd been force-fed smushed peanut butter and jelly sandwiches then kicked in the stomach.

"Very thoughtful of you. Just set them over there." Mrs. Schuster pointed to a shelf near the window. "I'll have my son put them in water when he gets back. Got to make him useful somehow. Still thinks he can tell me what to do." The words sounded grumpy, but her eyes twinkled.

Dad chuckled. "Being a son myself, I'd guess he's pretty worried. I'm just your neighbor, and I was pretty worried."

Mrs. Schuster cleared her throat. "Well. I didn't invite you here to listen to an old woman's complaints. The nursing staff fills that role just fine. If I may, I'd like to speak to Annie and Jason alone. I have something I need to tell them."

My dad glanced at Jason's, who nodded. "We'll be right outside if you need us."

"And keep that nosy son of mine out there, too." She winked.

When the door squeaked shut, my heart clattered in my chest. Heart attacks weren't contagious, were they?

"Thank you. For finding me, I mean." Mrs. Schuster licked her lips. "If this had happened two months ago, I'd be dead."

I could only stare. All those years of her screaming at us kids, I'd never thought about how lonely she must have been. My nose prickled and I knew tears wouldn't be far behind if I wasn't careful. But I refused to cry. I'd done enough of that last night.

"What happened?" Jason asked. He didn't sound like his usual shy self at all. But then, he's the one who'd kept his head last night. He was the real hero. It must be a law of nature that once you save someone's life you can't be shy with them.

"Heart attack. A minor one. Nothing a few more medications can't fix. But this is boring adult talk. I want to talk about the map and Cap'n Black Marge."

I felt sick. The one thing I didn't want to talk about. Of course it's the first thing she brought up. Another of nature's laws. Nature obviously had a sick sense of humor.

I stared at the tubes taped to Mrs. Schuster's wrist. To

the blood that filled the first inch or two. Should I admit I'd read the letters or just play along?

"I lied," Mrs. Schuster said.

My breath caught. I hadn't expected a confession.

Jason just stood there.

"Cap'n Black Marge isn't real." The snap in Mrs. Schuster's eyes faded. She seemed to sink farther into her pillow. "I — I made her up, hoping you'd visit to hear her story." She paused. A smile cracked her lips. "Wow, I sound pathetic, don't I? It's the schoolyard all over again."

I choked a laugh. "Why? You didn't even like us before. Why did you want us to visit now?" Okay. I'd read the letters. I knew the answer. But I wanted to hear her say it.

Mrs. Schuster sniffed. She sat there for a long time, staring off into space. Just when I was going to say something, she snapped back to reality, throwing a glance at the door. "I haven't told anyone this. Not even my son."

I didn't dare move. I didn't want to do anything to make Mrs. Schuster change her mind about telling. Jason squeezed in closer.

"Where to begin?" Mrs. Schuster sighed. "I have a granddaughter who's just your age. I didn't even know about her until this summer."

"How could you not know about her if she's ten?"

I elbowed Jason. "Let her talk!"

Mrs. Schuster chuckled. "They say laughter's the best medicine. I can't tell you two how good you've been for me.

"Anyway. Here's the short version. When I was fifteen, I left home. Sound familiar? I'm Marge. Her story is mine. I just embellished the details a little. So I married Leonard when I was seventeen, but he turned out to be a lout. Abuse and other things you don't want to hear about. When I found out I was pregnant, I left." Her face hardened. "No money, no place to stay, and I didn't even have a high school diploma. I wanted to keep the baby, but I had nothing. And I couldn't go home. Not with Pappy and his liquor."

I scooted closer.

"So I found an agency that specialized in helping girls in that situation. A place to stay, food to eat, and three golden hours with my daughter before the adoptive parents took her. Two weeks later, the agency sent me off with a little money in my pocket, and a big, empty hole in my heart."

I hung on every word. It was like one of Mom's soap operas, only real. I had to jump in. "Your daughter was the treasure, wasn't she?"

Mrs. Schuster nodded. "I spent years trying to find her. All in secret. My Edward, Ned, had such a tender heart. I should have told him. That's my biggest regret."

"Isn't giving up the baby your biggest regret?" Jason looked confused.

I elbowed him again. "Jason!" Even *I* knew better than to ask a question like that, which was saying something.

Mrs. Schuster laughed. "You two . . . No, it took me

a long time to get there, but giving up my daughter was the right choice. She's happy. She had a happy childhood. That's the most any parent can ask." She paused, and her shoulders slumped.

"Recently, I found her. Hired a private detective. Thing is, she didn't want to see me, which I can't blame her for. I'd prepared myself for that. But it was a blow learning I have a grandchild I'll never meet." Her voice was barely audible.

I couldn't hold it in any longer. I pulled the letter from my back pocket and laid it in her lap. "I found this last night."

Mrs. Schuster unfolded the wad of paper. She stared in shock. "You knew?"

I nodded. "The letters were scattered on the floor last night. When I picked them up I accidentally read part of the first one. I knew your husband wasn't Leonard, and you only had a son. I just wanted to understand. I know I shouldn't have read your . . ."

"Then you don't hate me?" Tears welled up in Mrs. Schuster's eyes. The papers trembled in her hands. "I never meant to deceive you like that. I convinced myself you were just playing along, enjoying the hunt . . . until you mentioned Jason's house. That's when the guilt set in. I wanted to tell you. I even tried a couple times, but I was addicted to your company, and I didn't know how to tell you without losing you." She wiped at her face. "I know I don't deserve it, but I humbly ask for your forgiveness."

I pulled a tissue from the box on the table and handed it to Mrs. Schuster. "I forgive you. And not just because you're on your deathbed, either."

Mrs. Schuster snorted, then coughed. Her trembling hand wavered in front of her mouth with the tissue, but I could tell she was smiling.

Jason shrugged. "I never believed you anyway. All grown-ups lie. It's like your brain chemistry changes when you turn eighteen and you can't help yourself or something."

Mrs. Schuster wheezed and started coughing again. I tensed to get help until I realized she was laughing.

I giggled until the beeping monitors sped up. The screen flashed red. Jason and I were halfway to the door when it swung open and a sandy-haired man rushed in. He looked familiar with his neatly trimmed beard. I could almost place him.

"Mother! Are you okay? What are you . . . are you *laughing?*"

Tears streamed down Mrs. Schuster's face again, but this time with laughter. She waved her son away, shaking her head and wheezing in obvious glee.

"It's not funny, Mother. Do you *want* to die?"

Jason nudged me and gave an ominous look. He pointed subtly at the man, then rubbed his thumb over his fingers. The universal sign for money. Horrifying recognition struck.

Two nurses bustled in. One focused in on Jason and

me even though we'd flattened ourselves against the wall. "I'm afraid you two will have to leave." Her voice was stern.

We fled, grateful for the excuse. We needed to be gone before Mrs. Schuster's son came out again.

Grabbing my dad's hand, I pulled him toward the elevators. "We should . . ." But it was too late. The door opened and Mrs. Schuster's son slipped out. I caught a last snippet of Mrs. Schuster's voice before the door closed.

"Now I'm not allowed to laugh, either? Next it'll be breathing!"

"She acts like we're out to . . ." The son's voice trailed off when he caught sight of us. His jaw, neatly trimmed beard and all, dropped.

I pretended to be fascinated by the lone purple tile on the floor where I stood. But I could feel him looking at me.

"These are your children? . . . My mother's rescuers?" His voice sounded unsure. I dared a peek. His gaze flicked from Jason to his dad, and I could practically see the wheels turning. He remembered us. I prayed he wouldn't say anything. Wasn't it bad enough he'd refused to help?

"Mr. Parker, you said?" Jason's dad nodded. "And Mr. . . ."

"Jenkins." My dad finished for him.

"You have extraordinary children. In fact . . ." The man scratched his head. "This is a bit awkward, but I'd like to thank them. I don't suppose they mentioned a certain trip to the . . ."

I stiffened. I shook my head, trying to beam the message to stop. But Jason cracked.

"We went to the bank!" His wild eyes reminded me of a cornered cat.

I slumped. So much for being welcome at Jason's house.

Our dads looked blankly at Jason. "The bank?" Mr. Parker asked.

Mrs. Schuster's son cleared his throat. "Let me introduce myself properly. As I said before, I'm Scott Schuster, Mrs. Schuster's son. But I'm also vice president in charge of lending at First Regional Bank of Northern Utah." He extended his hand, and when Mr. Parker didn't reach for it, my dad did.

"I had the pleasure of meeting Annie and Jason last Monday. They visited a branch of our bank requesting . . . ah . . . requesting mercy for a certain loan." He glanced at my dad, but addressed Mr. Parker.

"I see." Jason's dad spoke through clenched teeth. I cringed at the anger he was able to convey in those two words. I scooted behind my dad.

"I don't want to get them in trouble, sir. In fact, they were most charming. Gave a glowing report of the loan holder's character."

"Really?" Mr. Parker looked surprised, which was a nice break from the glare he'd been giving Jason.

"Most definitely. In light of what your children have done for my mother, I'd be willing to look more closely at their request. Though I can't make any guarantees without looking at the file, I'm fairly confident we could find a workable solution if the loan holder so chose."

I couldn't believe what I was hearing. I jumped out from behind my dad and grinned at Jason, who grinned back. He could stay! I wanted to shout for joy, do cartwheels down the hallway, and wave a victory banner from the roof. Jason could stay!

Mr. Parker rubbed the back of his neck. "I — wow, this has been a day of miracles. I'm speechless at your offer. It's extremely generous. But as the loan holder, I have to decline."

My ears rang with Mr. Parker's words. Cold washed over me and I shivered through my jacket. "You what?" I couldn't have heard him right.

"It's funny — crazy — really. We had an offer on our home yesterday. Bianca and I were waiting for everything to clear before we told anyone."

"I can respect that." Mr. Schuster shook hands with him.

My dad held out his hand as well. The traitor. "Congratulations, Ted! That's wonderful news."

"I give Bianca the credit. She keeps the house so beautiful. I know California's far," he spoke to Jason now, "but family's there. And we'll be together. This offer's a chance for a fresh start."

Jason gave me a look. A pitiful look that was a whole speech without a single word. I'd been friends with Jason my whole life. I knew what he meant. What he was asking. My heart sank. I gave a quick nod, then looked away.

"It'll be okay, Dad," Jason said.

His words burned in my ears. I couldn't speak. My throat was too full of tears. I stared at the floor, where the purple tile lay all alone. And I knew exactly how that tile felt.

"Though you declined my offer, I'd still like to do something for Annie and Jason to say thank you," Mr. Schuster said.

I wiped at my drippy nose. My life as I knew it lay in ruins around me, but an iPhone could go a long way in terms of comfort. I held my breath.

"I'd be pleased to have your permission to set up long-term, dividend-yielding stocks in their names."

26

I stared at the cookies and juice on my desk. No way I'd eat them. Jason's farewell was no reason to party.

Jason and I had made a PB&J pact. Shook on it and everything. We agreed to pretend nothing had changed right to the end. That way we could enjoy our time more. But a farewell party made it hard to pretend.

When the class mothers had served all the kids, Mrs. Starry stood at the front. "First, I want to thank Mrs. Pierce and Mrs. Lyons for offering their time and goodies for our little farewell party today. Class, what do you say?"

"Thank you" chorused through the room. Mine might have been mumbled.

"Second, Jason, would you please come up here for a minute?" Mrs. Starry beckoned, smiling far too wide for the occasion.

Jason was as red as jam when he got there. He stared at the floor and I could hardly blame him. Just because he was moving away was no reason to humiliate him.

"On behalf of the class, I wanted to wish you good luck on your move. I'm certain you'll succeed wherever you go. You've been a model student and it's been a joy having you in the class. We'll certainly miss you."

"Thanks," he mumbled and scurried back to his desk. Poor guy. Lucky for him he wouldn't have to face any of these kids again. But that was the only lucky thing.

"Now class, please, enjoy your cookies and be sure to throw your trash in the garbage when you're finished. The dismissal bell will ring in five minutes."

When Mrs. Starry sat down, Lila leaned over. I was surprised since she'd barely acknowledged my existence for the past month. Not that I was complaining.

"I'm really sorry he's moving, Annie. It stinks to lose your best friend."

I kept waiting for the insult to come, but she had clearly finished. "Thanks," I finally said.

Lila picked at her cookie. "I didn't mean to sound selfish. I just didn't know."

My face got hot at the memory. Not my best moment. I swallowed. "I'm sorry I said that. It wasn't very nice."

"Still, I deserved it." She paused. "I know I'm not Jason, but maybe we could do something . . . together . . . sometime?"

I didn't want to be rude, especially with her mom in the room, but I didn't want to make a promise I'd just have to break. Nice that she'd apologized, but that didn't change things. She was still Lila, and I was still me. I shrugged "Maybe . . . sometime."

Lila nodded and turned back to her desk.

I was relieved when Mrs. Starry called my name. "Annie, can you please help Jason clean out his desk? Grab the bottle of cleaner and get some paper towels from the sink."

I jumped up, nearly spilling my juice.

Jason already had his backpack out and was pulling the stuff from his desk. If this had been my desk, this project would have taken more than a couple of minutes, but Jason was a neat freak. Mrs. Starry hadn't been lying about that "model student" thing. Not that I'd ever say that to Jason.

While he divided his stuff into three piles (one to take home, one to throw away, and one to return to Mrs. Starry), I wiped out the inside of his desk.

"So what was Lila saying to you?" Jason hefted the pile of books to take to Mrs. Starry.

"Just that she's sorry you're leaving. And she asked me to do something with her. But don't worry, I'd never betray you with the likes of her."

Jason shook his head. "Annie, doing stuff with others isn't betraying me. I think you're wrong about Lila. You should give her a chance." He glanced over by the door where Mrs. Pierce stood, then lowered his voice. "Did you know the Pierces offered to buy our house, too? That same day we found out about the other offer."

My mouth dropped open. "Seriously? What'd they want with it?" A month ago I'd have guessed it was to plow it down to build a swimming pool. But since the food donation project, I had new respect for Mr. and Mrs. Pierce. Even if I wasn't fond of their offspring.

Jason knelt down, pretending to fiddle with his shoelace. He surveyed the room like the expert spy he was. When he spoke, I had to strain to hear. "Mr. Pierce called it a no-interest loan until my dad found a job. He said it was Lila's idea. Said 'My little girl would never forgive me if I didn't try.' I overheard my parents talking about it on the Spy Bud Two Thousand."

I was speechless. I stared at the back of Lila's head. *She* had done *that*? I didn't want to believe it, and if I'd heard it from anyone else, I wouldn't have.

I turned back to Jason, but he was gone. He was talking to Mrs. Starry at her desk, going through the books and signing them in.

It was all too much. My head was spinning with the change that never seemed to end. Hating Lila had been a constant in my life almost since they moved in. Now I'd lost that, too.

The bell rang, and the class exploded in a flurry of motion, stacking chairs and grabbing coats.

"Bye, Mrs. Starry!"

"Bye, Jason! Good luck!"

Kids called farewells as they rushed out the door. The whole thing felt like a dream. Or rather, a nightmare.

I closed my mind to it all and took my time wiping off Jason's desk to wait for him. We had less than twenty-four hours left together, and I planned to spend every second that I could with him.

27

Grrrr. I pushed the ruined slices of bread away. As silently as possible, I pulled out two new ones. It was still dark outside, but it was getting lighter. I had to hurry.

This was my third try. I dipped the knife in the peanut butter and concentrated on spreading it smoothly without tearing or smushing the bread. Plus I had to be careful not to contaminate the peanut butter with bread crumbs. Making a perfect sandwich was more difficult than I'd thought, especially in the dark. If it had only been Dad, I'd have risked turning on the light — he could sleep through an elephant stampede. But Mom was home — she'd traded shifts to help the Parkers clean house last night. And she would wake up if a grasshopper sneezed.

When the peanut butter slice passed muster, I pulled out a separate knife for the jelly. I couldn't taint the jelly. Not *this* time.

It was hard to stay focused. To not think about *things* — like the last soccer game Jason and I played (we'd lost, no surprise); our last trampoline war (I'd won, no surprise there either); our last Halloween together (we'd gone as pirates, duh). There were too many "lasts" to count. Which I hated.

My eyes kept trying to cry on me, but I refused. Besides, I didn't want to ruin another sandwich.

I glanced at the clock. It was late. I banished all thoughts except sandwich-making.

I broke down the purple globs inside the jar, then scraped them onto the bread. I spread it to the edges, covering every bit of white. To remove the excess, I ran the flat of the knife over it. No lumps. I laid the peanut butter side over the jelly side, and done.

Whew. I finally dared to breathe.

Ever so gently, I put the sandwich on my mom's best serving tray along with the flashlight, the freshly scrubbed hand shovel, and the folded-up note. The last touch was a fancy cloth napkin to cover the tray.

Once I had my coat on, I carried it outside.

Frost covered everything, and my breath puffed out in clouds. My feet swished through the leaves that covered the grass — leaves Dad would probably make me rake later that day. At the garden's edge, I hesitated. All the plants had been torn out and the dirt tilled the week before. The now-barren site felt lonely. I shivered to think this is how I'd feel all the time now, but I shrugged it off. Jason wouldn't be gone for a few more hours. I had to enjoy it. After all, we'd shaken on it.

I left the tray by the cemetery, then sprinted to Jason's house, only pausing to stick my tongue out at the moving van in his driveway. A flick of my wrist and a pebble chinked against Jason's bedroom window.

I had to throw three more before Jason peeked out. Another few minutes, and he stood next to me, shivering in his housecoat.

"Come on," I said. "I've got a surprise."

Jason pulled his housecoat tighter and frowned at his slippered feet. "At six in the morning? Can't it wait?"

I rolled my eyes. "If it could wait, would I be standing here throwing pebbles at your window? Now, come on!" I moved toward my house.

"Will it take long?"

I glanced back. Jason hadn't moved.

"My parents are already stressed enough. If they wake up to find me missing . . . especially after . . . well, you know. They'll . . ."

"They'll what?" I folded my arms. "Ground us from each other again?"

Jason laughed. "Fine." He stepped toward me. "I just don't want them to worry."

"They won't. We'll be fast. I promise."

Making sure he followed, I ran straight to the garden. Jason froze at the edge. He glanced at his slippers. "You didn't tell me we were coming *here*. I would have worn shoes. And where will I sit? My mom will kill me if I get muddy today."

Out loud I groaned, but inside I smiled. It was *so* Jason. Exactly the stuff I was going to miss. I rolled my eyes again before the hurt could hit. "Go barefoot then. Feet wash just fine." Marching to the cemetery, I took off my coat and spread it in Jason's spot. My mom would be mad too, but some things are more important than dirt. "You can sit there."

"Are you sure?"

"Jason!"

"Fine. Sitting."

I knelt by the platter. Moisture seeped through the knees of my pants. I ignored it. "I hereby call this meeting of the PB&J Society to order."

Jason sat up straighter.

Deep breath. I stared at my hands, willing my voice not to crack. "This is our last chance to bury a sandwich together. So it should be special. Mean something." I whisked off the napkin and grabbed the flashlight, pointing it at the sandwich.

"I hereby present the sacrificial sandwich and propose that a ninth and final rule be added as follows to the Smushed Peanut Butter and Jelly Burial Rules." I took the note from the tray and unfolded it. "If approved, Rule Number Nine shall be written into the books as follows: 'Thou shalt bury a perfect peanut butter and jelly sandwich if either of the two founding members moves away. It shall be called the sacrificial sandwich.'

"'This burial shall be a reminder of their peanut butter and jelly friendship. Neither the jelly nor the peanut butter is complete without the other. Just like us.' All in favor, say 'aye.'"

"Aye." Jason raised his hand and so did I.

"All opposed say 'nay.'" I looked around as though crowds of people surrounded us, then nodded in satisfaction. "The 'ayes' have it."

"So how does this work?" Jason wrapped his arms around himself, and I realized how cold I was, too. I stuffed my hands in my armpits.

"Exactly the same, but different. After digging the hole, you inspect the sandwich and declare it to be perfect. We both spit on it at the same time, then follow my lead on the rest."

"Okay, but we have to hurry. My parents will be up soon."

"We'll be quick. Now let the ceremony begin." I held out the gleaming-clean spade. Granted, it was hard to tell in the dark, but *I* knew it was perfectly clean.

After Jason dug the hole, I presented him the sandwich. He inspected it. Front to back, then around the sides.

He looked at me for approval and I nodded.

"I declare this sandwich to be perfect?"

It sounded more like a question than a declaration, and personally, I would have added a few flourishes to the statement, but I supposed I could let it slide.

Jason held the sandwich between us. I took one side, and when I'd built up enough saliva, I held up one, then two, then three fingers. We spit. Jason's gob struck my hand, but I didn't say anything. I couldn't. It was the rule.

Instead of laying the sandwich in the hole, I signaled Jason not to move. With the sandwich still between us, I read the modified sermon from the paper: "Our dearly beloveds, we are gathered here today to say goodbye to our friend."

It was like those words made it all real. A lump stuck in my throat and I didn't think I could go on. I clamped my mouth shut and thought about broccoli casserole as hard as I could. Because I would *not* start blubbering like a baby and ruin the whole ceremony.

I took a deep breath and continued.

"Though it totally stinks to be torn apart by rotten circumstances, we'll never forget the adventures we've shared: discovering penguins in Africa; the loss and recovery of the Christmas pigskin; conquering the enemy during the Second Great Turkey Battle; solving the mystery of Black Marge's treasure; not to mention the daring rescue of Margaret Schuster. I could go on, but I won't because a *certain* person is worried he'll get in trouble."

I improvised the last line, but I thought it worked okay. "Like this peanut butter and jelly sandwich, our friendship is perfect, too. The peanut butter is the glue and the jelly keeps things hopping. They complete each other."

Though I hadn't named names, I thought the descriptions were pretty obvious.

I leaned toward Jason. "Time-out. We have to pull the two sides apart. Just don't rip the bread."

Jason frowned. "But then it won't be perfect. And by the way . . . glue? You're comparing me to glue? They use old horses to make glue."

I bit my lip to keep from laughing. This was the ceremony. This was serious. I just needed to get rid of the image in my mind of Jason's face on the body of an old horse. "I meant it in a good way. And trust me on the sandwich. Time-in."

Raising his eyebrows, Jason gripped one slice and I held the other. We slowly pried the sandwich apart until we each had half.

The experiment worked better than I'd hoped. Each half looked pitiful. Slightly mutilated, and definitely not pure. "The pieces of bread can be separated or torn apart, but neither half will ever be the same. The peanut butter side still has jelly on it, and the jelly side still has peanut butter on it. Just like our lives. Though you're moving a bajillion miles away, you'll still be a part of my life. You always will be."

I had to force out the last words. Stupid tears were threatening again. *Broccoli casserole, broccoli casserole, broccoli casserole.* I wouldn't cry.

My hands shook while I stuck my half in the hole. I motioned for Jason to do the same. All too soon the hole was filled, the song was sung, and the moment of silence was over. Jason and I looked at each other. Our last adventure was done.

All the fun was gone. Neither of us smiled.

Finally, Jason stood to go. Immediately he dropped back to his knees. In a swift motion he wrapped his arms around me in an awkward hug. I squeezed back, breathing in everything about him. All of it: his melon-scented curls, his loyalty, his chipmunk cheeks, his constant worrying, his bravery and hard work, his patience. Especially his patience.

"Promise you won't bury any sandwiches without me?"

I wanted to laugh. As if I could even find a new friend who would understand. And besides, it was a rule. "I promise."

28

After Jason left, I sat in the cemetery a long time. I watched the sun rise, brightening the drab colors of night. The grass sparkled with dew. Patches of yellow and red autumn leaves reminded me of traffic lights. Usually I loved this time of year. But today, it felt like an insult.

Dark clouds should have covered the sky. Flowers should have drooped. The leaves should have all fallen to the ground.

In that moment, everything felt hopeless. I wished I could wake up and have it all be just a really bad dream.

"Annie? Are you out here?"

It was my dad. I knew I should wipe the dirt from my jacket and get out of the cemetery, but I couldn't move.

"Annie? I've been calling for five minutes. Why didn't you answer? And is that your mother's crystal serving tray? What are you . . ." His voice trailed off when he saw me. He knelt down and wrapped his arms around me. "Oh, sweet pea. You're so cold."

I clung to him like I hadn't since I was five. All the tears I'd been holding back gushed out. I let my dad's warmth surround me, filling the emptiness that had been growing over the last month.

Even when I finally stopped crying, I held on, afraid my world would collapse if I let go. Afraid my dad would disappear, too.

"Does it ever stop?" I asked.

"What do you mean?"

"Everything keeps changing. Mom's job, Mrs. Schuster getting sick, now this. I just want it to stop."

Dad chuckled. "Life *is* change. If nothing ever changed, the world would be a sad, sad place. Getting to know Mrs. Schuster was a change."

"But that was a good change."

"And it hasn't been *so* terrible having me around, has it? Maybe this will be like that. The good there, just waiting to be found."

I wiped at my nose and sat up. I wouldn't win. Dad was way too optimistic sometimes.

"So I was thinking we should make French toast for breakfast, and I bet the Parkers would like some, too."

"You won't burn it?"

"Are you questioning my cooking?" He stood and dusted the dirt from his knees.

I shook the dirt off my coat and pulled it on. "I'd just hate to be remembered for burnt toast, that's all."

"I suppose it's good your mom's making it, then."

I'd forgotten that Mom would be home and awake all day. I managed a smile.

Dad picked up the crystal tray. He tucked it under one arm and offered the other to me. "Shall we go in?"

Together we crossed the yard and climbed the creaky back steps. Inside, the smell of cinnamon filled the room.

Matt and Kate sat at the table with a pile of French toast in the middle. Mom was at the stove, still cooking.

"I *told* you she'd be out there," Kate said.

"Morning, honey." Mom kept her eyes on the skillet. "We'll let your brother and sister eat while we run some over to the Parkers. Just be sure to save us some." She pointed a warning finger at Matt, who grinned wickedly.

"Hey, you snooze, you lose." Matt stabbed two pieces and dropped them on his plate.

"Matt."

"Geez, I'm kidding. I think you've been working too much, *mi madre*."

The whole scene felt so normal. I had a hard time believing this was the worst day of my life.

I held the ziplocked plate and we left to say our last goodbyes. Next thing I knew, we were in front of the Parkers' house handing over our offering. Dad helped Mr. Parker load the last of the suitcases. Mom chatted with Mrs. Parker, waving away thanks and exchanging pleasantries. I stood next to Jason, suddenly not sure what to say. I'd already said everything in the cemetery.

Then I remembered my promise.

"Did I ever tell you my Slurpee-sipping secret? It's why I didn't get brain freeze."

"You managed to keep a secret from me?" Jason rocked on his feet.

I nodded. "I only pretended to drink so you would go too fast."

"But . . . that's cheating!"

"How?"

He opened his mouth, then closed it. "Well, it was sneaky anyway."

I grinned. "Like an expert spy?"

We fell into silence until Jason asked the question I'd been trying to avoid.

"Think we'll ever see each other again? California's pretty far."

I slugged him in the arm. "Of course we will!"

Jason rubbed his shoulder. "I won't miss that."

I ignored him. "Plus, you're going to e-mail me."

"E-mail isn't the same."

His negative thoughts would jinx us both. What was he going to do without me? "*And* I have a plan."

"You do?" Jason looked nervous.

"Disneyland's in California, right? So I'll just go online and put my parents on a bunch of mailing lists for Disney brochures. I'll have them convinced by summer for sure."

He nodded. "Your plans are getting better."

I was about to slug him again when his dad approached.

"Sorry to interrupt, but it's time to go. I want to get there by tonight, if possible." He eyed me. "Do you think our secret angels will know to stop delivering food?"

I squirmed, but my mom jumped in. "I'm sure they'll figure it out. Whoever they are."

Mr. Parker nodded. "Well if you ever discover who did it, be sure to tell them thank you for us. Times a thousand or so. That might almost cover it." He held out his hand.

I shook it firmly. "I'll keep my eye out."

"All right, say your last goodbyes. It's time to go." Mr. Parker jingled the keys.

Mom gave Jason's mom a hug. "Take care, Bianca. And let us know when you get there."

My face suddenly felt hot, and Jason's turned red. We both stepped back.

"Don't forget to e-mail me," I said.

"And don't forget your promise about the . . . you-know-what."

"Never." I stuck out my hand. "Peanut butter?"

He grinned and grabbed my hand. "Jelly."

We each clapped our other hand over the top and shook the PB&J oath one last time. There was no going back.

Jason's dad climbed into the moving van. Jason followed his mom to the car. When both vehicles disappeared around the bend, Mom put her arm around me.

"You okay?"

I stared at the corner where the cars had vanished. My ears buzzed, and everything looked a shade duller. But now was no time to be a sissy. I had a plan to carry out. Swallowing back what felt like a whole glob of smushed PB&Js in my throat, I took a deep breath.

"Do you realize we've never been to Disneyland?"

ACKNOWLEDGEMENTS

Much like PB&J, writing a book is a sticky business. And over the years, as I've worked toward getting published, all kinds of people have left their flecks of peanut butter in my jelly. (Oh yeah, I'm totally the jelly.) ;)

So, with Annie and Jason's approval, I hereby propose SPB&J Rule #10: A sacrificial sandwich may be offered up to individuals in order to show respect or appreciation. As such, I offer a gigantic one to the following people, and induct them as honorary members of the PB&J Society:

First, my agent, Victoria Marini, who worked tirelessly to find the right home for my story. Her passionate belief in it kept me going when I wanted to give up.

My editor, Donald Lemke, who laughed at all the right spots, and who understood the importance of PB&J from the beginning. I couldn't have asked for a more perfect editor match. Who knew edits could be so FUN?!

Brann Garvey, Senior Graphic Designer, whose vision for the cover and general book design exceeded all expectations. One of my new favorite pastimes is staring at the cover.

And everyone else at Capstone who had a hand in ushering this book out into the world. Including my proofreader, everyone in marketing and publicity, the production crew, and those in printing. Thank you!

Brenda Drake, who sponsors Pitch Madness and who tirelessly supports other writers and helps them achieve their dreams. Dee Romito who pulled my book from the Pitch Madness slush pile and is now a friend and trusted confidante on this crazy road to publication. And Erica Chapman, who selected my book for her Pitch Madness team. Without these guys, I never would have connected with my agent.

Sarah Barley and Laurel Garver, whose thoughtful and encouraging critiques pushed me to make that last crucial revision that led to getting an agent.

My Virginia Critique Group — Julia, Heather, Carolyn, and Megan — who painstakingly read the thing chapter by chapter when the story still needed A LOT of work. Thanks for believing in the story, even then!

The Firehouse Five — Tessa, Lisa, Victoria, Jane, and Angela — who generously let me back in the group and who have been there to cheer and commiserate with me every step of the way. Love you guys!

Amy Sonnichsen, who not only read my book, but kept me sane by encouraging my inner silliness with Hacky Sack Videos, ice cream eating contests, and the like. Hacky Sack Club Forever!

Sarah Schauarte, Rebecca Sumner, and Patricia McCleve, who all took the time to read and comment on early drafts.

And of course, Becca, Mike, Paul, and Kim, who inspired so many of the events in the book. Our childhood rocked! (And because I can't resist — Neener, neener! I got McDonald's and you didn't!)

Janet and Wayne (a.k.a. Mom and Dad) who always believed in me and taught me that I can accomplish anything I put my mind to (even if it takes ten years or so).

London, Brandt, and Khyah, who are my everything. Who patiently waited for me to "finish one last sentence" too many times to count. And who make me feel like a rock star by bragging about me to their friends and to every stranger they meet. I love being your mom!

Rick, who listened to my horrible rough drafts and gave honest feedback even when I didn't want it. Who hugged me at those worst moments, and did the happy dance with me at the best. Thank you for always inspiring me to be better. Forever or bust, baby!

And finally, the real-life Jason. My first ever best friend who, despite his ill-fated move when we were five, left the globbiest of peanut butter globs in my life. The memory of that glorious, crazy friendship was at the heart of everything I wrote.

JANET SUMNER JOHNSON

Janet Sumner Johnson lives in Oregon with her husband and three kids. She bakes a mean cinnamon twist and eats way more cookies than are good for her, which explains her running habit. Though her full-time occupation as evil tyrant/benevolent dictator (a.k.a. Mom) takes most of her time, she sneaks in writing at night when her inner funny bone is fully unleashed.